Set in the Cumberland countryside,
Breed of Giants tells the story of
Josh Johnson, a farmer, who breeds
his gigantic Shire horses and, with
almost fanatical devotion, brings them
up to championship status, only to
have his hopes shattered by an accident
to his best horse and an outbreak of
foot-and-mouth disease on a
neighbouring farm.

How Josh copes with his burdens and
builds once more his winning strain of
Shires, is told with all Joyce Stranger's
skill and charm.

Also by Joyce Stranger

THE RUNNING FOXES
RUSTY
ONE FOR SORROW
REX
ZARA
CASEY
CHIA THE WILDCAT
LAKELAND VET
WALK A LONELY ROAD

and published by Corgi Books

Joyce Stranger

Breed of Giants

Illustrated by
DAVID ROOK

CORGI BOOKS
A DIVISION OF TRANSWORLD PUBLISHERS LTD

BREED OF GIANTS
A CORGI BOOK 0 552 09893 0

Originally published in Great Britain
by Hammond Hammond & Co. Ltd.

PRINTING HISTORY
Hammond Hammond edition published 1966
Corgi edition published 1968
Corgi edition reissued 1973
Corgi edition reissued 1975

Corgi Books are published by Transworld Publishers Ltd,
Cavendish House, 57–59 Uxbridge Road,
Ealing, London, W.5.
Made and printed in Great Britain by
Hunt Barnard Printing Ltd, Aylesbury, Bucks.

I owe thanks to many people.

To Mr Roy Bird, Secretary of the Shire Horse Society of Great Britain, for his help and interest.

To Mr J. M. Frazer, Divisional Veterinary Officer, Ministry of Agriculture, Fisheries and Food, for information on veterinary matters.

And especial thanks to Mr James Gould, of Lymm, without whose help I could not have written this book.

Those who breed horses will know him as a famous judge and a breeder of many champions, among them Lymm Sunset and Lymm Lady Grey; Lymm Grey Friar and Lymm Grey King.

They will know today's champions; Lymm Sovereign, Lymm Patch, and Lymm Powisland Black Prince.

They will have watched that magnificent stallion, HIS EXCELLENCY, take pride of place as Shire Personality of the Year at Harringay, in 1957.

May the breed never die.

This book is pure fiction from beginning to end. None of the people exist; and none of the places. Many of the incidents concerning the Shire horses were told to me, and are based on true events. There is no pack like the Horton pack and no truth in my tale.

PREFACE

In many parts of England men are still breeding Shire horses. Not just one man, or two men, but quite a number of them, all dedicated to preserving a part of England's tradition.

'Why keep the breed alive?' I was asked while writing my book.

To which I can only reply, 'Why keep England alive? Why have a Queen, or a King, or preserve a historic castle or an ancient cathedral, or a beautiful picture, or a lovely view? Why bother to live at all?'

Too many sweeping reforms are destroying the old ways. Not all of them are good ways, but on the one hand people complain that we have nothing to offer the world in the way of tradition, which is nonsense; on the other they clamour to do away with Well Dressing in Derbyshire, with the Welsh Eisteddfod, and the Manchester Whit Week Walks, when the children of the churches of Manchester, dressed in white, parade through the streets, accompanied by ceremonial police.

This, the moderns claim, interferes with commerce, and makes traffic control difficult, and passing through the city impossible. We must progress, make way for the motor car, make life easy for everyone, so that there is no longer struggle, nor difficulty, nor triumph in overcoming either. In the end nothing will be left but modern motels and holiday camps and miles of macadam motorway, while the visitor from abroad goes away to find a country that still has a heart and a soul.

7

The men who breed the Shires know this only too well. They are keeping tradition alive. They are men with a mission to fulfil, and they have joined together, leagued by the British Shire Horse Society to try to see that not only does the breed survive, but that it survives in all its beauty, unmarred by faults that might weaken it.

These horses are thought to be the descendants of the ancient war horses, the sturdy British horses that drew Boadicea's chariot, armed, on its wheels, with knives of wrath that mowed down the invaders.

These are thought to be the direct descendants of the horses on which the Knights of Chivalry went out to battle, thundering, man and beast, in full panoply of armour, terrifyingly, across the sward, as champion met champion in noise and shock and din. Only horses like these, built on a giant scale, could have borne the mass of armour worn by both.

These are the descendants of the beasts that drew the ploughs; that dragged the wagons up the slippery hills, that pulled the drays for the brewers, that were kept by carters, whipped and suffering, before the R.S.P.C.A. began to make a land that was fitter for an animal and rules that ensured that horses were fed decently and housed properly and rested thoroughly and were not beaten.

These, their descendants, groomed and fêted, the proudest feature of every English Show, in Peterborough and Blackpool, in Warwick and in Windsor, to name only a few, are bred for beauty and strength and nobility, and bred to remind us that once England depended on them, along with their cousins, the other heavy horses, the Suffolk Punch and Clydesdale, for without them there would have been no transport, but it was these, the Pride of the Counties, that earned themselves the counties' own name of Shire horses.

Few of those who have seen the Shire Personality of the Year, standing splendid in the spotlight at the Horse of the Year Show, dwarfing the heralds' more delicate mounts, will ever forget the giant horse, proud and handsome, head held high, mane brilliant with tiny standards, tail braided with ribbons, his harness gleaming, a tribute to his owner's care and pride.

All horses are regal creatures, but the Shire is surely King, and there are many men today conscious that he must keep his pride of place, a living testament dating back to the Blind Shire of Packington in 1755, who is the known ancestor of our modern beast and was himself the descendant of a long line of forebears that made England's history possible.

Too many crimes are committed in the name of Progress, crimes that are not acknowledged and can never be punished. I hope that the Shire Horse Society will never draw a line beneath its records, and write beneath it: 'On this date the last Shire horse of England died. The breed is now officially extinct.' For that also would be a crime.

And that is why I wrote this book.

CHAPTER ONE

BRUTON-UNDER-THE-WATER had always had reason for
pride, for this small Lakeland village boasted much that was
old, and much that was good, and much that was beautiful.
The stone cottages crouched in the lee of humped dark hills,
long lines of fells sweeping away to Horton Pike, high on the
far horizon, and down to Hortonmere, and the larger village
of Horton itself, beyond.

In the *Swan* at night, under the blackened rafters, half
hidden by rank pipe smoke, the men met and argued, bet
and laughed and drank, each man with dog or hound at
his feet, and his beer mug in his hand.

Mrs Jones, the placid, buxom landlady, her homely face
merry, went among them, her tongue quick to voice acid dis-

approval of noise or nuisance. There was no bad behaviour in the *Swan*. By day it was famed for home-cured ham, for apple pie sweeter than a dream, for pie and pudding and pasty, and rum butter, and Jersey cream from the wise old cow in the orchard.

In winter the Hunt met for teas at the *Swan*, after a day on the fells following the hounds on foot, each man bringing his own beast and betting on it. Come evening, at the *Swan*, they argued the merits of their respective hounds, each one bragging of sire and dam and vowing to breed and train a hound that would always be first at the kill and first home after a drag.

In summer Bruton came into its own in another way, for its major attraction was the Bruton Shires, and visitors from all parts came to see them. Josh Johnson, of Tedder's Leigh, was a man with a mission, a dedicated man, a man who lived for horses; his family, ever since anyone in the village could remember, had always bred the splendid eighteen-hand Shire horses, who were, many contended, the best of the English heavy horses.

'Talk that Josh is going to have to sell up,' Jo Needler said one late spring night, sitting over his beer in the *Swan*. Jo was an undersized, henpecked man whose nursery garden barely made a living for him and his shrew of a wife and his ailing children. The latter were always sick with bronchitis or croup, a snivelling pair detested by the villagers but tolerated, for the Needlers were local folk, born and bred in the place, both of them.

'Sell up?' The Colonel, a rare visitor to the *Swan*, was sitting at the big white-scrubbed table. There was no public bar. The men sat on oak settles in the vast old kitchen, where a two-gallon copper kettle was forever a-boil on the hob, and the landlady's kittens sprawled on the bright pegged rug in front of a log fire and spat at the friendly hounds and dogs.

Colonel Horton, almost Squire, who owned many of the farms and holdings, was shocked by the news. The men were mildly uneasy at his presence, best behaving, glancing slyly from face to face.

'So it's said.' Ted Wellans, a big, comfortable man, was the largest landowner apart from the Colonel. His was a rich farm. His house, old as the *Swan* and steeped in legend, was reputed to be haunted in more ways than one. On occasions the bathroom door jammed fast, no matter if lock or bolt or even the door itself was changed, and the youngest child was afraid to venture alone, even with electric light, down the stone-floored echoing passages and up the creaking dark oak stairs to bed.

The Colonel sat frowning. Josh owned his own land. The Johnsons were an ancient family too, but times were bad, horses expensive to keep, especially the big Shires, which weighed a ton and ate a fortune every week.

'Bruton without the Shires would be unthinkable.' The Colonel, a fair, stocky man with a moustache that bristled defiance at the world, now looked at the men who sat around the table, roughly dressed in their day-by-clothes, some leaning on an elbow, others with legs a-sprawl, most of them quietly contemplative, sucking at their pipes, tamping tobacco, faces briefly glowing in the glim of a match as they lit and relit, forgetting to draw on the stems as they listened and argued.

Heads nodded agreement. The Shires were more than a tourist attraction. They were a part of village life. In a place where most men kept farm animals of one kind or another, all felt they could comment on the breeding of Josh's horses. They would also speculate on the possible prize-winners at the shows, commiserate when a beast failed to win, and re-joice with Josh in yet another red prize ticket to pin on the wall of the harness room, among the enlarged photographs of former champions and the newspaper clippings.

The children adored these horses, visiting them on the way home from school, tiny fists offering clumps of grass, torn from the headgerows, that were always accepted by the big

13

friendly beasts, all of them good tempered except for the Bruton Jet. He was a notorious rascal, likely to bite or kick given half an invitation. Josh kept him apart, but the animal had his own ways of joining his half brothers; he was able to open a gate, and, incredible to anyone who knew horses, was unafraid of the electric fence, unhitching it and walking through, scared of nothing in the world except loud noises.

Favourite of all was the grey dapple mare, Bruton Silver. Always eager for company and conversation, she yickered to the children, galloping over the meadow to accept not only grass but ice cream and jelly babies and dollie mixture. She would hold out her tongue for the delighted little ones to coat with the coloured baby sugar icing shapes that they themselves loved, and they would stand and watch while the colours spread and mottled her mouth. When she had had enough she would swallow dreamily. Josh had, reluctantly, to make a rule that she was not fed too often, as she could never have enough of this sticky treat.

Bruton Cloud, a fine grey stallion, had, the year before, endeared himself forever to the men who were digging a trench across the field for a water main leading to a group of new houses on the other side of the village. At lunchtime he came among them and asked to share their sandwiches, nudging those who were reluctant to part with food with a hard and urgent head. A horse that proved to have a taste for roast beef and cheese and pickles caused so much amusement that he earned a paragraph in the local paper, and visitors came prepared to tempt him with yet stranger fare, so that Josh had to move him into the far field, lest his diet prove too much for him.

The Colonel, listening to the men recalling other endearing absurdities, to the talk of past Shires, also famous in their own ways, thought of the very well-known Bruton Emperor, Supreme Champion – was it '46 or '47? No matter, he ended up as Personality of the Year at Harringay, a marvellous horse, and some of Josh's present Shires were descended

14

from him. The Colonel frowned at the thought of Josh's difficulties.

'Remember Bruton King? Devil of a horse. Trampled a groom. Spiteful beast. Before the war, that would be.' Jo Needler emptied his mug and looked hopefully at the Colonel, who nodded to Mrs Jones. Froth creamed over the edge of the mug, and Jo's hound put his head on the table and licked at it greedily.

'The Jet's the same breeding. Accounts for his temper. Vicious streak in that line. Comes down from Black Satan – about 1919, he'd be.' Mrs Jones did not remember personally, but her father had often spoken of the horse, and she took as much interest in the Shires as the men. She'd grown up in the days of horses, of the great beasts that pulled the drays in her father's time at the *Swan*. They would pull up the street on icy mornings, to stamp and snort and steam outside the inn while the men in their padded jackets hauled the great barrels across the pavements and sent them rolling down the wooden ramp through the hatchway in the wall into the cellar beneath. Afterwards the men would come in for a drink and one of her mother's apple pies, which they shared among them. The brewery still bred greys and showed them – beautiful beasts. Pity if they were allowed to die out because nobody could afford to breed them.

The inn door swung open, and Ned Foley breezed into the room. Once a tramp, now respectably housed and almost a reclaimed character, he still contrived an odd air of raffishness, his dark jacket torn on one pocket, a vivid tartan scarf vying defiantly with a green-and-blue-checked shirt, a thin wisp of grey beard, new-grown that winter, decorating his chin. Each hound waited impatiently for a word from the little man as he passed, tails thumping a welcome. Ned had a way all his own with animals, almost one himself the village reckoned, with a beast's quick instincts, and a love of the night, and a need to keep to himself, and a fellow feeling for every creature that walked, or swam, or flew.

'Talking about Josh's Shires,' Jo Needler said, making room on the settle. His hound forsook its master and leaned a loving head on Ned's knee, gazing soulfully into the man's lined face with brown-eyed adoration, stern wagging amiably, thumping against the table leg.

'Best Shires in the country,' Ned said solemnly. He grinned suddenly as a thought crossed his mind, his mischievous Puck-face alight with laughter. 'Saw the Sable and the Ebony as I came along. Lying under the trees. Josh's cats were sitting on them. Ginger one on Sable's head, tailless one on Ebony's shoulder, and little one sprawled along Ebony's back, paws hanging down on either side. Proper sheepish, those two great horses looked.'

There was a subdued chuckling, but the Colonel laughed out loud, a hearty bray that made the men relax and the rafters shake.

'Where is Josh?' asked Ted Wellans.

'Brooding,' Ned answered, a small frown adding more lines to his seamed face. 'One obsession after another. Drives Peg mad. A man that waits for bad luck. Seen a magpie today. One for sorrow, he says.'

'Who hasn't seen a magpie? Nobody shoots them any more and they're breeding all around the place. Court bad luck, and it comes.' Mrs Jones gathered up the empty mugs, a woman who had no time for superstition. 'All of us'd be underground of despair if we believed all that old rubbish.'

'Don't need to look for ill luck, not with horses.' The Colonel knew his subject. There were three hunters and a racehorse in his own stables, and he had just nursed them through a nasty dose of equine influenza. The racehorse mare, in foal, was still causing anxiety, and the vet came daily, involved, as he always was, with every patient, whether large or small. The Colonel would pay well, but Dai Evans would give as much time to a child's pet rabbit and never grudge a minute.

There was little more talk. The Colonel drained his mug,

16

nodded a brief good night, and walked into the cool evening air. A thin rain pattered on the leaves. His thoughts were active, and he strode fast. His retriever was close at heel, a friendly, biddable dog, well trained, and brilliant in the field, with a mouth soft as butter when he brought a dropped bird.

The Shires *must* stay in Bruton. How, the Colonel did not know. He knew only that Josh must go on breeding them, showing them, travelling with his champions from place to place, so that a tradition should not die. Progress killed too many good things. Old houses, no longer homes, stood roofless or sheltered offices. Churches, famed for their grandeur, rotted and fell or were condemned and pulled down to make way for supermarkets, all glass and tiles and tasteless processed breakfast foods.

The Colonel's step quickened to march time. Behind him came the phalanxed ghosts of a million horses – horses of plough and farm and haycart; wagon horses and dray horses; gallant horses dragging gun carriages over field and furrow over plains, up hills and into valleys, wise eyes and brave heads and gallant muscles pulling, pulling. Their hooves thundered in his mind, the great horses of England, the Pride of the Shires, from Sussex to Suffolk and Norfolk to Devon, through lakeland and downland and on fell and on mountain, giant horses on whose broad backs England rose to glory.

As cloud thickened and rain swept over the fells, blotting out Hortonmere, the Colonel paused to look down on Josh's farm, just below him. The Shires of England – so few now left, so few men who wished to breed them, rear them, feed them; so few men like Josh, who cared nothing for luxury or money, but cared passionately for their horses, never able to resist adding yet another to the farm.

The Colonel turned his coat collar high to shelter his face from the rain that drove against him. The dog, wet and miserable, plodded on dourly. The Colonel toyed with one idea after another, yet none of them seemed feasible. He might help in small ways, but there was nothing he could do on a bigger scale.

Long before that summer was over the Shires seemed fated to disaster, and Josh, always superstitious, developed a major obsession that threatened his peace of mind almost beyond endurance, caused, absurdly, by a harmless wild creature that had the whole village quarrelling.

The Colonel, anxious for the Shires, aware that perhaps he alone was fully concerned with their importance and their history, came almost to despair, seeing yet another line of breeding becoming extinct, because if Josh sold up, who would buy the horses? Few men were left who had time or money to keep them.

They might be gelded for working – but how many farms still used heavy horses? And then they would not breed. If only he could buy them himself – but he was already over-committed. The future lay in Josh's hands, and the Colonel could only move behind the scenes, trying to provide an assured future, without Josh ever becoming aware of the fact that there was someone working for him, helping, unseen and unknown, for Josh was a proud man, and the knowledge would have hurt him beyond words.

CHAPTER TWO

TEDDER'S LEIGH, Josh's farm, lay to the west of Bruton-under-the-Water. It was good land, though not so rich as Wellans. There were wide acres where the mares could foal and roam in peace, and where, out of sight of them, and beyond the house, the stallions could browse in the buttercup-studded meadows. Sometimes, when the moon was hanging low in a star-spattered velvet midnight sky, their heavy hooves could be heard for miles as they cantered, moon-struck, thudding over the grass.

The Bruton Jet had been entered for the Cantchester Show. Fed like a king, his diet boosted with cod-liver oil to make his coat shine, his eyes were bright, his head high, his shoulders proud.

Only that day Josh had stroked the broad brow, pushing

19

aside the fringed hair that fell over wise brown eyes, and shown off his beauty to Rob Hinney, the cowman from Wellans.

'Look at him! Four years old. Eighteen hands. A perfect stallion. Best I've bred yet. It's in the bag.'

He was jubilant, anxious that everyone should admire the way the Jet stood, the movement of his legs, the sweep of head and back, and the silk of mane and tail; but for all that Rob frowned, and Peg Johnson, had she heard her man, would have told him to hold his whisht. It never did to count the apples till the blossom was set, not even Josh, whose Shires won more prizes than any others in the County.

That night Josh gave a rare treat of sugar to the stallions when he checked the fastening on the five-barred gate. There was a special catch to make sure they did not release themselves, but it did not always lock. He made sure it was caught and firm. He ran his hand over the deer stakes along the top bar, nailed palisade-wise. Deer would jump a gate but never a palisade fence, and he did not want them stealing his grazing.

He watched the stallions for a moment, as they shifted slowly, dark shadows under the shady oak. The night was noisy with their breathing. Tomorrow the Bruton Jet would go to Cantchester. All plans were made. The wagon was booked. Fare and entry fees were paid. A win at Cantchester would give him confidence for the all-important Royal.

Two more days, and then Josh could show his favourite's paces in the ring, savour the approval of the watching crowd, feel breathless excitement as he waited for the Judges' verdict, the only verdict that could possibly be his. Repayment for years of breeding, of choosing mare and stallion, of picking the foal, of feeding him, gentling him, training him. Repayment for long hours spent the night before the Show, watching over him, grooming him, braiding mane and tail with shining ribbons until he was fit to walk before the Queen, who might, herself, be there.

Later that night, remembering other Shows, and the roar from the throats of the bystanders as the winners were announced, he smiled into the shadows of the moonlit room, lying sleepless with anticipation in his bed, his wife breathing heavily beside him.

It was quiet in the meadow. Dreamy with darkness. A tiny wind riffled the grass heads. An owl called, mourning the lack of prey. Its wailing note roused the Bruton Jet. He moved majestically into the moonlight, head bent to crop the grass, his shining bulk black against the brilliant gleam.

Old Brock was restless. Wandering underground, he was exploring the earth where he had been born. He had returned to it from far away, where men and dogs had troubled his resting place and killed the little sow that had been his mate for years. He was lame, suffering from a deep cut on his paw.

He was hungry, but he would not find food underground. He ambled on, a broad-hipped little bear, striped head turning, when there was room, from side to side, until at last he pushed his nose into clear air, sniffed dew-wet grass, crushed thyme, and bruised clover, and the sudden alarmingly unfamiliar horse scent.

He backed swiftly, shoulders filling the tunnel behind the sett opening. The Bruton Jet was close to him, unstartled. The wind that smoothed his coat did not reveal the smell of badger, and his head was up, eyes watching the vague threatening shape of a roosting owl that in his turn watched the grasses for movement that betrayed mouse, or mole, or the unwary wandering chick of a pheasant.

The badger was not the only hunter prowling that night. Although he retreated to his sett, and lurked at a safe distance from the entrance, another animal caught his scent, and came running swiftly, anxious to still the hunger that savaged him.

Ruff was a collie, black and white, with a torn ear, a matted coat, and two wild eyes that showed only fear. He had been born in a remote hut on the hills, brought up with kick and cuff and harsh curses until one day, after a savage beating, he left his home and began to forage for himself on the moors.

It was a good time of year for a hunting dog, for there were young hares and rabbits, chicks of pheasant and grouse and partridge, ducklings on the ponds, and mice and moles in plenty. That night he had eaten a mouthful of frog, a dish he despised, had fought a fox and lost, leaving it to eat its own kill, and high on the moors, had chased a lamb, but left it alone in the end, not yet wicked enough to kill sheep.

The strange badger scent might mean a good meal. He paused in the moonlight, looking down the hill. He wanted to make sure that the place was free from man. Man who kicked and cuffed and swore, shouting at his sensitive ears. He eased a sore shoulder. Man, who shot.

A shepherd had seen him chasing the lambs, and aimed carelessly. Ruff was not badly injured, but the wound was painful, he was slightly lame, and he was a step nearer to sheep-killing.

The badger smell was new to him, alien and intriguing, borne on the wind. It excited him, and he crept forwards, legs bent, body close to the ground. Brock caught his scent and vanished completely, never to use that exit again.

Ruff skirted the Shire, having no fear of horses. He knew the wild ponies, out on the moors. The Jet caught the scent of the dog and turned and huffed noisily. He hated the creatures.

The badger had gone. The collie was wild with youth and hunger and plain mischief. He ran, barking, at the big hind hooves, taking care that the horse did not turn fast enough to sight him. He yapped, and the Jet tried to trample the dog, avoiding the snapping teeth and snarling mouth. The collie jumped forward, sighting on the soft feathering above the hind hoof, and bit.

He bit through skin and muscle, through nerve and sinew. The stallion pawed the air, rearing, in pain. He screamed, a terrifying sound, as he tried to kill the devil that had attacked him. His backward kick caught the collie on his sore shoulder and he fled, whimpering, racing through bracken and clutching bramble, jumping the ditch, pushing through the hedge, and speeding to safety high on the moors, where he could hide in peace, untroubled by horse or man.

Josh heard the noise and came running, coat and trousers dragged hastily over spotted sky-blue pyjamas that his wife had made from remnants bought frugally at the winter sales. His red hair and beard were tangled with sleep. The plunging stallion towered above him, and he knew better than to approach. He leaned on the deer-proof gate, talking softly, until his voice reminded the Shire that men brought comfort, and he limped, bleeding and trembling, towards his master.

Josh led him to the stable, lit the lamp, and whistled in dismay when he saw the damage the savage teeth had made. He left the horse and went to the phone, and Dai Evans, roused from his own sleep, promised to come at once. Josh returned, busying himself with cloth, disinfectant, and warm water, and cursed his bragging tongue, for the Bruton Jet would not now be able to enter for either Cantchester or the Royal, and might never be fit again.

If he were lamed. . . . Josh punched one fist into the other hand and swore.

'Comes out of counting apples,' he said, as Dai came blinking out of the darkness.

'Counting apples?'

The Vet was half asleep. He rubbed his eyes, yawning. He bent over the hoof, gripping the Shire's leg between his knee blacksmith fashion.

'No Show for him. Lucky if he walks foursquare again.'

Gentle hands bathed the cut, filled the syringe with penicillin. A few pats and the needle went home, the top screwed in hastily as the Jet plunged in fear.

'He's fierce,' Dai said. 'Not like the Bruton Cloud: do anything you like with *him*.'

23

'The Jet's the better horse,' Josh answered. He tugged angrily at his beard. 'Thought it was in the bag.'

He did not add that he had high hopes of his horse being unbeaten champion and Personality of the Year at the Horse of the Year Show. That secret ambition was best left unvoiced.

'What bit him?'

Dai was packing his bag, his hands slow and his eyes heavy with the need for sleep. The night before he had helped a cow to calve for most of the dark hours.

'A bite, was it? *I* wondered if it was men. Funny things, a man will do, and I sacked a hand last week. Left Silver on dirty straw and never reported her cough.'

Dai yawned and nodded. Bruton Silver was the best of the two mares, and also a champion. She was due to foal, later in the year, and a cough would need extra care. He looked wearily at the lambent moon, riding up the sky above Hortonmere, which lay sombre below them, moonlight fingering the dippling water.

'That's a bite,' he said. 'Big teeth. Bigger than a dog, I reckon. Could be a dog. Doubt it though.'

He yawned again, crashed the gears, clumsy with tiredness, and drove away, red tail-lights eyebright for half a mile down the long narrow road.

Josh gentled the Shire and gave him a feed of hay to soothe his temper. The black horse stood uneasily, his bitten leg eased beneath him to rest the weight. Josh sighed deeply, saying goodbye to his hopes of a championship, slid hard fingers lovingly down the muscular neck, and dimmed the lamp, which faded to a soft glow before it died.

It was no use trying to sleep. Peg might worry, but he could not answer questions, not tonight with his greatest hope so newly shattered.

The ground was cold under thin slippers. Behind him the solid greystone house bulked large and squatted under the hill, shining windows winking back at the uncaring moon.

The three Shires left in the field were dark bulks in the shadow beneath the tree, sheltering in uncomplaining silence, waiting for the day.

None of them ready yet for the Royal. He looked them over, trying to distinguish colour in the blackness. Bruton Ebony. Bruton Sable, visible because moonlight brightened his three white socks. And Bruton Cloud. All young. Perhaps ... Next year ...

He lit his pipe, tamping tobacco hard, wreaking futile anger with stubby fingers on the dry dead leaves that filled the bowl more than halfway. His head bent, he shielded the flame and it flared, caught, and faded, the match as dead as his hopes. The familiar taste brought slight relief as blue smoke wreathed his head and eddied slowly skywards.

Old Brock was still hungry. His striped face was sharp against dark earth. The horses scented him and moved away. Josh watched him run, weasel-swift, yet clumsy, downwind, coming out of the ground outside the field; almost in the farm garden.

'So that's the feller,' he said to the darkness. 'Be after my chickens next.'

He went indoors for his gun. His wife was waiting, the kitchen fire dancing with new-burning logs. She looked at him, her face anxious.

'Badger bit the Jet.' He was terse, avoiding the sympathy in her eyes.

'Is it bad?'

'Aye. He's out of the Show.'

Peg Johnson had her wisdom. She poured her man a drink to warm him, and he, only suddenly realising how cold he was, put his feet to the blaze and eased himself into the big creaking chair. A kitten began to purr and his tight mouth relaxed, and he forgot his gun.

That night Old Brock found a terrified leveret, crouched frozen, feigning death. It twitched an ear as he approached, and he seized it, killing swiftly. Farther along the trail he marked a mouse, and took it, and despoiled the domed nest, made of grass laid stalk by stalk in round perfection.

Full fed, he limped back to his sett. Day splintered the sky with silver and then patched it with scarlet streamers that reflected dully in the wind-tossed lake and the dark puddles left by a sudden morning rain.

He avoided the field where the stallions waited for their rations, and, deep underground, he slept, curled nose to tail, forgetting his throbbing paw. Above him, men worked, and the Bruton Jet nursed pain and black bad temper, and limped on his swollen leg and was put in the field alone, lest he harm his companions.

And Josh cleaned his gun, wondering if his horse would ever win another Show, or would, if the Fates were cruel, need a shot himself to end his pain. He looked towards the heaped earth of the badger sett and vowed vengeance.

CHAPTER THREE

Next night the badger avoided the stallions' field. He limped, dog-like, on three good legs, holding the injured paw high, nursing it carefully. It had been cut, almost to the bone, by a shard of glass left carelessly on the moors. It was healing cleanly, but the sinew had shortened. Old Brock would always be lame.

He ambled along the dark tunnel, conscious of damp earth close against his thick fur, and of noise and vibration above, as the stallions shifted their grazing ground. He waited, listening, aware of light and shifting shadow, of the wind sighing in the trees, bringing him news of a roaming fox, of herded cattle browsing or sleeping, of sheep, and of horse. None of these meant immediate danger.

Brock was hungry and also thirsty. He eased himself out of

the sett, scratched thoughtfully, shook his body to free the fur of dry grains of clinging earth, and then passed, without heeding, the piled-high bedding that he had shifted and replaced three nights before. He padded noisily down the hard-beaten badger track towards the stream.

He grunted as he went. Once, pausing to look at wind-stirred bushes, he was seized with ecstasy, with the pleasure of being alive, of wandering in the dark and chilly night, and of the immediate prospect of satisfying his thirst. He yelped, an eerie unnatural noise that startled a rabbit and sent it skittering through tussocky grass to an adjacent burrow.

The stream was shallow. Moonlight glinted on clear water that sparkled over sharp rock and rounded boulders. Chuntering water-noises were companionable and familiar in the shadow-patched night. A trout lay, nose to bank, drowsing quietly in the shelter of an overhang.

As Brock came noisily down the path, the fish flicked its arrowed silver body and darted for the safety of the willow-shaded pool on the farther side, where no animal came to drink because of the steep bank and the depth of the dark water.

The badger looked around him, and bent his head, disturbing the wavering image in the ripples. At the least sound he lifted his muzzle, glancing up and down, right and left, wary and wild. Bright drops fell from his jaws and gleamed on his whiskers. When he had done he shook himself and blundered into the shallows, where he cooled his throbbing paw and eased hot pads. A fox, questing down-wind, saw him, and changed direction, preferring to pass unnoticed in the night.

Pushing himself awkwardly up the bank, he crossed long shadows of close-growing trees, listening carefully for the sound of man or dog, his nose ever ready to warn him of danger. He knew where he was going, knew the beaten track, the gap in the hedge, the shallow pit beneath the wire under which he could crawl, and the enticing furrows of soft earth that held young turnips. He had sampled them, long ago, in his cub days, and the memory was still sharp.

Brock pushed through the gap in the hedge, bending rag-wort and loosestrife and foxglove beneath him so that the broken stems bore witness to his passing. His claws scored the bank as he scrabbled under the wire, and then he found himself surrounded by surfeit.

The earth was soft, and broke easily, so that he needed only one paw to dig out the turnips. He ate noisily, taking the tender parts, leaving some half-eaten, breaking leaf and stem of the plants as he trod carelessly, browsing happily along the furrows.

Glutted, he left havoc behind and retraced his path. The walk had made his foot painful again, so that he was thankful to reach the shelter of the tunnelled sett and the haven of his resting place. Clean bracken and gathered leaves and grasses made a soft bed on the hard-packed earth.

That night, in the *Swan*, Ted Wellans complained bitterly about the damage wreaked in his turnip field, and sympa-thised vigorously when Josh told of his own disappointment. Stories were bandied about other badgers, and the crimes they had committed. Ned Foley listened, frowning. Jasper Ayepenny patted his dog and brooded disconsolately into his beer-mug, only half listening. The new schoolmaster, drinking a shandy beside the fire, interrupted suddenly, and the men stared.

'A badger wouldn't bite a horse,' he declared.

Josh drained his mug, wiped a hand across his mouth, and then stroked his beard. He was in a wicked temper, and ready to fight anyone that provoked him. Today he should have been at Cantchester. Tonight another man would be work-ing on another Shire, a Shire that would win the trophy that should have been his.

'So you know all about badgers,' he said.

Mrs Jones, drinking a cup of tea, one of the kittens on her lap, intervened hastily.

'Now, Josh,' she said. 'What's done's done, and it's no use fretting.'

'And a badger did it,' Josh said. He glared at the schoolmaster. 'Town-bred, ain't yer, mister?'

It was an insult, and meant as such, and the schoolmaster, who had only been in the village for three weeks, flushed, and swallowed awkwardly. He was young and unused to country men, or to any men much older than himself.

'Don't sound like a badger,' Ned Foley, more famed for his poaching than his work, felt sorry for the schoolmaster. Proper fish-out-of-water, and daft to send a man like him to a place like Bruton, Ned thought. And not the only one to think so, for Mick Stacy was bred in Birmingham and had never been farther from the town than Blackpool before.

'Saw the brute myself,' Josh said. He slammed his mug down on the table. 'Same again.'

Mrs Jones picked it up, and took it to the sink, which stood in a corner of the big stone-flagged, black-beamed room that served as kitchen and also saloon bar.

'Enough's enough, Josh Johnson,' she said, tempted to tell him acidly to mind his manners. Instead, she smiled at him to soften the blow. 'No more from me tonight, or I'll have Peg on my tail in the morning.'

'Hen-pecked!' Jo Needler grinned broadly, saw Josh's expression, and promptly regretted the remark. He said good night hastily, and made his way through men and beasts to the door. Jasper's setter, Nell, lifted her head to watch him go, and then pushed it at her master, wondering why he was so glum.

'Best go home,' Ted Wellans advised, but Josh sat on, his face dark, his mouth set in a grim line that meant ill to anyone who crossed him.

'I'll have that badger,' he said. 'If it's the last thing I do. Take the dogs and hunt it down. Be after our chickens next. Damned brute. That horse might be lame for life.'

He brooded over the fate of the Bruton Jet. The schoolmaster finished his drink and went out of the door, saying nothing. The Huntsman, who had been sitting silent in the corner, tapped Jasper on the knee, wondering if the old man's wits were leaving him. He had been strangely silent for the last week.

'Remember the badger down at Buttonskille?' he asked.

'Aye. And the one that killed Skim.'

The Huntsman cursed to himself. He should have remembered the old man's terrier, killed while rescuing two trapped hounds from an underground tunnel.

'Jasper, what ails you?' asked Mrs Jones. 'You're as crotchety as a cat that wants to go out at night and chase moonbeams.'

Jasper stood up, huddling himself into his coat. He flicked a finger and his gleaming red setter stood beside him, her head held proudly. She rubbed against his hand.

'I'll not be bothering you much longer,' Jasper said, with forlorn dignity.

'You'll live to a hundred yet,' said Ted Wellans, who owned the richest farm in the district. 'You're not ill, man?'

'I'll not live to a hundred here,' Jasper answered. 'The folk that knows 'ave condemned my cottage. Going to pull it down. They've a place for me in the Home in the big town. Come on, Nell, lass. You'll be having a new master soon.'

The door slammed behind him, and nobody dared follow him. The Huntsman took a long draught of his ale, swallowed the wrong way, and choked. He coughed violently, and when he had recovered his breath and his colour, he, most unusually, swore.

'It's a damned shame,' Ted said heatedly. 'Why the devil can't they leave the cottage for a year or two? The old boy can't last much longer. They might let him die in peace.'

'He'll die soon enough in a Home,' Ned Foley said. He stared bitterly at the fire. 'Like putting a beast in a cage, to take Jasper away from his cows and his chickens, and the fields, and the folk here. Pine away and die, like a bird, with nothing to live for. Just streets and cars and the stink of a town. What's Jasper to do with all that?'

'I'll be damned if they do that to him,' Ted said. He slammed his beer mug down on the table, hard. 'We'll do something about it. Who's with me?'

There was a rough noise of assent and approval from the men. The Huntsman took out a pencil, and Mrs Jones brought paper and they sat down to work out a plan of campaign.

Meanwhile Jasper walked slowly and forlornly up the hill, desolation in his heart. He stood at his gate, watching the cows shelter under the old tree, listening to the sounds from the brook that ran behind his garden, hearing a hoot owl call to its mate.

The gate creaked behind him. He walked up the well-worn path, the setter following close at heel. Everything had meaning tonight, much more so than usual. The awkward way in which his key fitted into the resisting lock, the swing of the door, the feel of the rug beneath his feet, the familiarity of his wicker chair, the noise Nell made as she drank from the bowl beneath the cracked stone sink, and the purr from Stalker, stretching out on the mat, almost too old for hunting, but well content to hug the fire and rest his head on his master's shoe.

The letter from the local council lay on the table. Jasper crushed it in a ball, then spread it out again. He knew every word by heart. He repeated them to himself, and then blew his nose vigorously, cursing himself for a damned old fool.

It was a long time before he found the will to go to sleep that night. Every sound was dear to him. Every hoot and whisper, every call from fox, and badger, spoke of finality. The last time. He would not hear them in the town. He would hear only the sound of cars and buses, of speeding trains, of busy people who did not care whether foxes ran in the woods, or badgers roamed free, or an old man died of slow starvation, his soul deprived of everything that made life good.

He dreamed of enclosing walls, and cried out in his sleep so that Nell came to him, licked his face, and then, as if aware of his distress, broke a lifetime rule and curled up on his bed, her head on his knee, while Stalker, looking for warmth denied by the dying fire, crept beneath the bedclothes, to lie undetected in the hollow of his master's back.

CHAPTER FOUR

THE lowering sky was midnight-dark, heavy massed thunderheads black above the fields. The far horizon burned, sulphur yellow and wicked. Lightning cut the world in two, flashing across the hills to flame and explode in an oak which sheered and split, one side falling to the sodden earth with a sullen crash.

The three stallions fled, to cower together in a grassy hollow, bodies pressed close for reassurance, tails into the wind, they bowed under the rain that drove against soaked hides and manes and that splattered in flinty sliding arrows on hard ground and soaked into turf and heather, making a morass in which hooves plunged and stuck.

In the farther field the Bruton Jet, always nervous, was maddened by terror. As the tree fell, he shouldered through the hedge, unaware of tearing spiny brambles or the strand of wire that caught his hoof, opening the half-healed bite. He yickered, bedevilled by thunder that pealed overhead, rolling from peak to peak, echoing on the hills in long drum-like syllables that crashed on, never-ending.

Josh, finishing a hasty and over-cooked meal, after a morning spent trying to bring in the hay before the weather broke, swore, and left the table, swallowing as he ran. Hooves pounded on the cobbles and the Jet whinnied in shrill fear as once more the terrifying light flared blindingly and died, leaving a darkness that was uncanny in mid-afternoon.

Josh opened the stable door and the horse turned into the sheltering familiar box, as the sky flamed again, flashing electric blue from horizon to horizon. The Jet stood, tail to the door, trembling, afraid of the din and glare of the noisiest storm for years.

Outside, in the distant field, the other three stallions came at the sound of their master's voice, glad of human companionship. They shouldered each other amiably, anxious to be first to greet him with outstretched muzzle, and to feel the reassuring hand that stroked and patted, bringing comfort.

The loose boxes were welcome. Josh dried sodden coats, quietened them with a word, and with hay that distracted them while thunder rumbled and threatened ominously, too close overhead.

Later, Josh walked over to the hayfield, and looked at the soaked unshifted bales, scattered over the stubble. It had been a good crop, and now, judging by the weather forecast, fully half would lie and rot. He turned, seeing a dog streak from the hedge and make for the hill. It was not one of his, and he ignored it.

Ruff had known snow and ice, the bitter discomfort of frost under his pads, the unease of wind, the terror of gales, and the searching misery of rain that soaked him to the skin. He had never seen lightning, nor heard thunder, and a faint hope of succour sent him to the farm, near to men, to shelter from the driving rain that stung his eyes and nose, and then, turning to hail, battered him mercilessly.

When he heard the Jet squeal, he crept between two bales that leaned against each other, leaving a crack that was partly protected from the weather. Here he crouched, until Josh came to look at the havoc caused by the storm. His courage failed, and he slipped towards the hedge, body low, hoping to remain unseen, afraid that the man might have a gun, like the shepherd who had injured him.

He did not stop, nor see the man turn back to the farmhouse. He ran upwards, over the squelching grass, over the boggy moss, over the flinty river-bed, dry a few days before, now surging with shallow brown foam-flecked water, and on to the bare hillside.

Here he paused, shaking water out of his fur. The rain continued relentlessly. Soaked and shivering, he sped up the hill, finding it easier to move with legs bent and body flattened, so that the wind travelled over him. Whites of rolling eyes showed his abject terror.

There was peace of a sort in a familiar cave, made by two flat rocks leaning together, angled to hold a third uneasily above them. The rain did not drive in here. He crouched at the back, listening to the demons that plagued the hillside, grumbling ruthlessly, deafening his sensitive ears. Paws over eyes, he shuddered at each lightning flash, unable to obscure the light which tore at his brain. He wanted comfort and companionship for the first time in his life, and did not know how to find it.

Later, when the rain had eased to a thin and miserable drizzle, the thunder had gone, and the sky had cleared to a milky grey that held water in its surly folds, he came out of his retreat, and drank from a rocky pool, shaking himself vigorously to free his fur from as much wet as possible.

Other creatures were creeping out. The dog watched a group of rabbits browsing on thin grass. They were wary, alert between nibbles, sitting up, ears pricked, listening, noses working to catch the first taint of alien scent borne on the wind.

The dog was away from them, well behind the wind, which drifted a warning. At once a hind foot thumped. The rabbits scattered, bounding to safety in burrows that led far underground, too narrow for the hunter.

Baulked of his supper, Ruff began to range the hill, hunger a snarling anger in his belly. He saw a hare, but she was far away, and the wind did not carry the tell-tale message that she also had two young. He looked towards the distant farm. There were ducks and hens scratching by the pond. There were lambs bleating for their mothers, some of them very young, for lambing was late on the fells.

Dusk was shadowing the peaks, softening the dripping

hills, masking the fresh-leaved trees. Ruff was urgent, craving food. He ran again, down through a wood where water dripped in incessant dreariness and a squirrel fled, chattering angrily, back to the high drey where he had been born.

The path led over rough rock and loose sandy earth, over black peat and yellowed spongy moss, through a hedge and across a field where a new lamb dropped, very late and unexpected, and the ewe bleated suddenly with the pain of birth.

The scent of blood was on the air. The lamb was staggering to its feet when the dog rushed in, jumping for the softness of throat beneath the chin. The cruel teeth bit deep, and the lamb died as the ewe roused herself, and, with the blind devotion of motherhood charged the dog.

Caught off-guard, he rolled, but turned and snapped and bit, so that she kicked, and then, as he flung himself to attack her, fell and, weakened, could not rise. He dragged the lamb's body to the ditch, and fed well.

When he was done, he left the carcase, and, sated for the first time for months, returned to the cave on the hill, where he lay and slept, curled nose-to-tail, warm and dry and comfortable, and twitched in his dreams.

Josh, walking through the sheep field, which belonged to a neighbour, looking for one of his own dogs, missing since the storm, found the sheep, and went to look for Nick Beston, its owner.

Nick was a small man, his face wrinkled with unending worries, mostly about things that rarely happened. He swore vigorously as he lifted the ewe, and tracked the blood trail to the ditch and found the lamb.

'Reckon it's the badger,' Josh said, his mind on his own misfortune.

Nick scratched his iron-grey head, pushing back a disreputable cap to do so.

'Dunno as badgers kill lambs,' he said doubtfully.

'Badger bit my Jet,' Josh answered, mulish.

'We'll set the dogs on it.' Nick shouldered the ewe. 'Didn't think that lamb was due for another week yet.'

They walked back together. Nick put the ewe in an old shed used during lambing time, bedding her on straw. Josh's dog appeared from inside, approaching his master diffidently, wagging an anxious tail.

'You old fool. Thunder don't hurt,' Josh said.

'Don't it then?'

Nick pointed to the tree. Silently they walked over to look at it.

'Good job there were no cattle sheltering under that,' Nick said, his face grim. He trudged back to see to the ewe, while Josh whistled his dog and went back to feed the horses and bemoan the fate of his crops to Peg, who was already measuring bran, knowing that he was late with his work.

CHAPTER FIVE

NOBODY saw or heard the stranger, running down the wind from Coniston way. He had been hunted five times the year before, and gone to earth high on the fells beyond Horton Mere. Cunning as age and nature could make him, he fed well until he was caught by a trap, and frantic with pain, hunger, and terror of the almost invisible bond that held him he chewed off his paw, and fled on three legs to hole up and heal himself.

The fox was surly with hunger. Passing close to the tattered wire surrounding Tanner's fowl run, he caught the wickedly delighting chicken smell.

Tongue lolling, mouth slavering, he soon found a way in, and a moment later the frantic hens were running in panic, while one of them, a fat speckled brown that laid good large eggs, was dead in front of him, her head bitten off.

He carried the body outside and fed well, crouched behind an untidy hayrick. Licking lips and chops, savouring the aftermath of pleasure from his food, he relived the moment of killing. It was a wild satisfaction, not to be denied.

He spent the rest of the night in the hen-run, and when he was too full to eat, he took his kills, and buried each one, dog-like, in the soft earth of a potato clamp, where Tanner found them a week later, and swore mightily, insult heaped high on injury.

Brock, following the track past the farm an hour after the killer had gone, caught the smell of fresh-killed chicken and dug up one of the still-warm carcases, and fed royally, leaving his tell-tale tracks all round for the men to find in the morning. The fox was well away, trekking back to the high fells, where he slept, basking in the sun, hidden by bracken that grew breast-high to a man, and that opened into a comfortable rocky place that caught the warmth and held it.

Tanner, finding badger tracks and dead hens, drew his own conclusions, and that night, in the *Swan*, the beer talking loudly inside him, he made plans for a badger dig the next evening, and the men excited at the prospect, began to remember other exploits.

'Sounds more like fox nor badger,' the Huntsman said. He, too, was glum, and Jasper was missing, his apathy preventing him from walking down to join the other men.

'Saw the tracks,' Tanner said. 'Trying to tell me I don't know fox from badger?'

'Foxes go on killing sprees, and bite off their victims' heads.' The schoolmaster had graduated from shandy to beer and was prepared to assert himself.

'Fat lot you know about it,' Tanner answered rudely, and Mrs Jones, slapping down a tankard in front of Ted Wellans with unusual force, turned and spoke sharply.

'No call for rudeness, now. Likely schoolmaster's read books about them. Tell you a lot, do books.'

'Books!' Tanner said, with supreme contempt. 'I know

41

what I saw, don't I? Trying to call me a liar?'

'Nobody's calling you a liar.' The Huntsman stood wearily. He was feeling his age, he was worried about Jasper, and he had had bad news himself, only that morning. Ranger, his hound, waited, his eyes on his master.

The men watched him, wondering at his unusual behaviour. It was not like the Huntsman to be moody. Jasper, now, he was quite unpredictable, and easily hurt, sensitive with the wariness of old age to insults that had never been intended.

The Huntsman nodded, snapped his fingers and went off into the evening cool, the hound following at heel, completely biddable. They took the road to the tops, hesitating at Jasper's cottage, but there was no sign of man or beast, except for Stalker, bird-watching through a window.

The Huntsman's thoughts were uneasy company. Mouth set, he eased his mind with walking, until he reached the high tops and looked out and saw his own private enemy. It came towards him, slashing through red earth and brown, surging through rock, striking, knife-like, across field and road and coppice, angled directly at his own cottage, that waited, an old and unwitting victim, for the final stroke to finish it.

The new motorway. He stared down, hating it, hating the drills and the explosives, the cranes and the bulldozers, the paraphernalia of progress. These were the killers, the men who destroyed grass and field and farm and grazing, wiping out with the crush of a heel the tiny life in the long grass, the place where the vixen schooled her cubs, their constant play leaving the grassy patches as bare as if a group of children had worn away the turf with heavy shoes.

In the name of progress they cut down trees that sheltered finch and hawk and owl, squirrel families, and skittering bats. In the name of progress the motor cars sped on their way, hastening to live tomorrow today, and leaving behind them the crushed bodies of rabbit and badger, of mouse and hedgehog, of hare and squirrel. Leaving behind them the torn and maimed bodies of men and women, and of children.

In the name of progress the cottage in which he had been born, and in which he had hoped to die, would be smashed, stone by stone, until nothing was left but a memory. The road would sweep through the quiet village street, widened to carry it, bringing the town in its train.

He looked away, over the rocky fells, where heather brightened to leaf and tight bud, and a hare loped easily up-hill, making Ranger whimper with eagerness, and look anxiously at his master, hoping for the signal to run.

The Huntsman gazed inwards, not seeing the hill, his mind far away, recalling the days long ago. He had been a real Huntsman then, had his own pack to train and breed, picking the best hounds for scent and song and speed and sense, the Master's approval sweet in his ears. They had been good friends, but the Master was dead these five years, and he himself had long surrendered his job to a younger, spryer man.

Now he contented himself with training the villagers' hounds, the younger ones, at this time of year, lacking drill, forming a raggle taggle. It was not the same. Nothing was the same.

Ranger, bored, and anxious to be hunting, pushed a cold nose into his master's hand.

The Huntsman had not seen the hare. He had not noticed the bracken, or the summer fresh new shoots of heather, or the wide cloud-speckled sky. Bitterness blinded him, and it needed the hound's urgent paw, sharp against his leg, to recall him to the present, and the fact that animals must be fed, even if man had lost his own appetite. He turned and plodded downhill, and Ned Foley, passing him, but out of earshot, saw the huddled figure go by, and thought sadly that Huntsman was showing his years.

Downhill, crossing the shallow water that bubbled from a rocky spring and splashed gaily over slimed grey rock, the

43

Huntsman noticed the newly enlarged earth made by the midnight visitor to Tanner's farm, marking it for next season's Hunt, before he realised, with sudden sickness, that he would no longer guide the pack.

Crossing the path beaten out by deer and badger, the Huntsman looked down on the field where the stallions grazed. The Jet, his injury part-healed, had been returned to run with his half-brothers, and he stood alone, tossing his head impatiently to try to rid himself of the flies that swarmed beneath each long-lashed eye.

He was irritable with heat, edgy because one of the dogs was lying in the shadow under the hedge, and goaded by flies. A clegg landed and stung him on the neck. Bruton Sable, grazing peacefully, drew level with him. He reared, and lashed out blindly with a heavy forehoof, catching the Sable on the withers.

The other Shire turned, moving swiftly for all his size. Before a man could twitch an eyebrow, the two stallions were fighting mad, wicked hooves striking out, mouths wide to bite.

Josh, busy in the milking parlour, heard them, yelled to Peg to take his place and finish scalding the churns for morning. He ran at speed, anxious to prevent his champions from harming one another. The Huntsman, knowing that one man alone would do no good, hurried down the path, his feet sliding on bare rock, Ranger following close.

'Keep the hound away. He hates all dogs,' Josh yelled, seeing him as he clambered over the drystone wall, running towards the stallions' field. The Huntsman signalled to his pet to sit and wait. Disconsolate, Ranger obeyed.

The field was noisy with hate. The Jet whinnied, high and furious, and Josh grabbed his mane and tugged, trying to pull him off the Sable, whose neck he had gripped with his yellow teeth. The maddened Shire kicked and squealed, and the Huntsman, running, breathless, took the Sable's mane and tugged in his turn, both men wary for kicking hooves.

The teeth let go, and the Sable, glad to be free again, and afraid of the hot blood that poured down his neck, danced heavily backwards and out of reach.

The Jet, thwarted, squealed, reared, and plunged. Raging, savage, and wild with fury, he buried his teeth in Josh's forearm, which was raised to catch him. The Shire bit to the bone, just as the Huntsman closed the yard gate, leaving the Sable standing head hanging, out of harm's way.

White with pain, Josh yelled, and the Huntsman hurried back, grabbed at a bramble stick projecting from the ditch and brought it down on the Jet's neck, forcing him to turn. He was beyond control, his eyes rolling, whites showing, his ears flattened, his mouth open and vicious. The cut of the thorny stick halted him, but not for long. Josh and the Huntsman moved fast, out of his way, over the wall, as heavy hooves pounded towards them.

'He's out of his mind. He'll have to be shot,' Josh said, nursing an arm that dripped blood, grim-faced, teeth set with pain.

Peg, looking out of the milking parlour, which she was hosing down, gave a small scream, and dropped the hose, and came running, unaware of water spilling over all of them. The Huntsman turned off the tap.

'He's always been wicked,' Josh said, looking at the magnificent mass of bad temper that raged over the field. 'Can you do the job?'

The Huntsman nodded.

'I'll fetch Ted Wellans' rifle,' he said heavily. It would be easier to shoot the beast when he had quietened down. Now, raging across the field, mouth wide open, ready to bite, he might botch the job as the horse stampeded towards him.

'Damn fool way to stop two stallions fighting,' Peg said, furious, as she examined the wound.

'Hadn't time to think. Did the first thing that came into my head,' Josh said, defending himself and wincing under her none-too-gentle fingers.

Peg tightened her mouth. Trouble with Josh was that he never did think. Went at everything bull-headed. And that led to trouble.

When she had bathed and bound the arm, Peg pushed her man into the battered old green soft-topped Land-Rover, that always smelled of pig and calf, and drove to the cottage hospital, where they kept Josh in for the night, adding injections to his soreness.

When the Huntsman returned with the rifle the Jet had exhausted himself, and was feeding quietly in the dusk. There was no pleasure in the task, and less in calling the knacker, but he killed the horse cleanly, and waited for Peg's return, knowing she would be forlorn. He had no words to greet her, and he waited until the knacker, philosophic, came into the yard, removing the body late that night as a favour, knowing Josh and Peg as friends.

'It's an ill wind,' he said, when he saw the size of the animal.

Peg said nothing. She slammed the kitchen door, and left the men to get on with the job. She had always been afraid of the Jet, but she hated to lose a beast, and she knew that they could not afford the loss.

She stood for a long time in the moonlit room looking at the over-flowing desk, full of unpaid bills for fodder and equipment. When at last she went wearily to bed she was conscious of every sound and tick and creak, and terrified by the noise of heavy breathing, until she traced it to Libby, the donkey, come to stand companionably close to the house and the mistress she adored.

There was little sleep in the night, and she woke tense and aching, thick-headed, knowing she must get on with the milking. She found the Huntsman bringing the herd from the field, and smiled at him gratefully.

He paused at the gate, seeing badger tracks in the wallowed mud.

'Aye, that's our ill luck,' Peg said, following his look. 'Be

glad when they put the dogs in. Mebbe the luck'll change.'
She thought of the bills on the desk. 'It can't get worse,' she
added, and clucked to Maybelle, as she took her usual place
at the head of the queue and went into the milking parlour,
her expression placid as she waited quietly for the cups to be
fastened in place.

CHAPTER SIX

JOSH came home with a sore arm, a sore head, and a sore heart. The Jet had been his pride, a certain winner, a future unbeaten champion at all the Shows. And worst of all, he had been too young to sire a foal, for Josh would put no mare to the stallions until they were four years old.

If only . . . The words tortured him. If only one mare were in foal to the Jet. All that splendour wasted.

'Better so,' Peg said, knowing his torment. 'We've never had one so vicious. His foals might have been as wicked.'

Josh found the Jet's pedigree, and looked back. Back to his father, back to his grandfather, and what he saw there sent him to the telephone.

'Aye,' said the Colonel, who knew the history of every Shire in the area. 'That was the Killer. Killed two grooms and crippled his owner before they shot him. He was a great horse, but man, he was a devil. Just as well your beast never sired a foal. Blood will out, and there's bad blood in that line. Any of the others from the same breeding?'

'Not one,' Josh said, thankful he had never put another mare to the Jet's father. Maybe good came out of evil, after all. None the less, he was going to get the badger, which brought the ill-luck. Might lame another horse.

He looked at the field where the Bruton Cloud was feeling his youth and rolling like a colt, huge white-feathered legs waving absurdly in the air, his coat glistening in the thin sunshine that barely pierced the grey above them. In another year he would have matured, become solid and splendid, put on weight. Perhaps next year. . . . Josh was an incurable optimist, his temper volatile, and Peg smiled to herself when, as she finished scalding the churns, she heard him walk across the yard and whistle 'Billy Boy', a sure sign that he was recovering from one of his black moods.

That night the men congregated in the farmyard, their faces tight with excitement. Jo Needler had brought a terrier with him, a rough-haired, darting creature that watched with bright eyes and head cocked and ears a-prick as the men busied themselves at the sett entrance.

'Is he down there?' asked Ted Wellans, looking at the tunnel that angled sharply into the ground, preventing anyone from seeing into it. So far as he knew, all other exits had been stopped.

'Heard him snorting, down in the dark,' Josh answered. He had been watching from dusk onwards, anxious that the badger should not escape, and unwilling to kill him with a shot when the men were wanting sport.

'Be better to gas 'un. Surer like,' Ned Thatcher said, gruff, shifty-eyed, remembering illegal trappings and snarings that he would not like found out. Unlike Ned Foley, who was never unnecessarily cruel in his poaching, and prided himself always on a clean kill.

'You'll not use gas on my land.' Josh hated gas. It was tricky stuff, too. Never knew what leakage there might be from the ground. There was an old tale, going the rounds, that might or might not be true, about a man who tried to gas a badger, far beyond Coniston, and failed to stop every hole. Gassed his own chickens, every last one of them, as the stuff leaked through a crack in the ground. And the badger survived, goodness knew how. Too tricky, gas was.

'We'll use the dogs,' he said, whistling up his own, and the three came running, little gentle collie Jess in the lead, only to go back, tail down, when Peg called her, not wanting her hurt.

Old Brock lay listening to the turmoil above him. Heavy boots thudded, shaking the ground, and the men shifted from place to place, sounding like a tramping army. At the first bark of a dog the badger sat, erect, eyes bright, ears listening, and head cocked in the darkness. He knew what was afoot.

A few minutes later he was heading out into the tunnel system, looking for an exit as far away from the men as possible. Long before the first terrier was down, he was digging through fallen earth to an exit no one had seen, far up the hill. Ears alert, he paused, listening, then eased himself through, and the soft soil fell in behind him.

The new section was unexplored territory, and he trotted warily. Beyond the fall-in the tunnel was firm and spacious, but he was a big badger, broad-hipped with age, heavily built, and his body had little room. The wall was close against his fur, grains of loose earth clinging. A graveyard scent of damp was all around him; so was the rank smell of fox, for an intruder had been visiting and left chicken bones behind him.

Brock came out of the tunnel twist that led to the entrance. He stood, savouring the air, his nose warning him of nearby rabbits, of a bird, roosting above him, of mouse and mole. He paused for several seconds before emerging, and Ned

Foley, lying up on the hill above him, grinned to himself as he heard the old badger stop and grunt and scratch busily before plodding along his own trail, out of sight. Below, torches flashed, spades thudded into the ground, a dog barked, and Ned hugged himself with glee.

Brock knew where he was going. He could use his half-healed paw, although he still limped. There were rabbit burrows on the side of the hill. In one of these four babies crouched, waiting for the doe, who had gone to feed.

The badger scented them, and began to dig. The helpless rabbits shivered, terrified, as relentless claws bit through the earth towards them, exposing their nursery to the sky, where an edge of moon showed pale against the void of night. Death came swiftly, and Brock, sated at last, pushed through the bracken and over the hill, his heavy rustling progress fading away, so that soon Ned lost all trace of him.

Below, the men were arguing. Ted was sure that the badger had escaped and the earth was empty. Ned Thatcher had gone away, surly, when excitement had failed to materialise. No one was sorry. He was cranky company at the best of times. Jo Needler put his terrier down, and the little dog romped through the tunnel and back, baffled by the strong scent which lay overpoweringly, yet led to nothing. He came out again and sat and whimpered.

'Tom fool dog,' Jo said furiously.

'Can't hunt what's not there,' the Huntsman said reasonably, having come to see what was happening. Ranger, beside him, snarled amiably at Jess, who must, Josh thought, have crept out again to see the fun. The bitch licked the hound's nose, and the terrier, finding better occupation than hunting invisible beasts, trotted across to the collie and nudged her. She turned, snapping, as two hounds nosed her, eyes bright, faces interested.

'Hey!' Ted looked hard at the animals. 'Going to breed hounds from your sheepdog, Josh?'

'Never rains but it pours,' Josh said crossly, and lifting the bitch up, locked her into a shed. Every dog in sight followed him hopefully.

A moment later there came a whine from the farmhouse.

'That's Jess!' Josh said, startled. He went to the shed. 'Whose bitch is this?'

Angry denials came from all the men as he took her from the straw.

'She's the image of your Jess,' Ted Wellans said, staring at the collie, the deception aided by the patched shadows in the windy yard.

There was a movement in the darkness beyond the gate.

'Who's there?' Josh's voice was angry. He wanted that badger dead more than he could say. Somehow he identified it with the luck of the Shires, and while it was alive he'd not handle any winners.

'Come out, whoever you are, or I'll fetch my gun.'

'Don't be a fool, Josh,' the Huntsman said testily.

Light from lanterns and torches and the open farmhouse door spilled on to the cobbles, throwing shadows that leaped and flickered and grew and faded as a man came towards them. The newcomer was almost level with the men before they recognised the schoolmaster. The strange bitch tore herself from Josh's arms and ran at him, jumping up eagerly, licking his face, uttering shrill whines and tiny excited welcoming yelps.

'No business letting that bitch down here,' Josh said, his voice deceptively gentle. Peg, knowing him, came out and stood beside him.

'Josh,' she said, her voice warning.

'Hold your tongue, woman. Now, schoolmaster. Is that your bitch?'

'I borrowed her,' the schoolmaster said. He grinned suddenly, his face mischievous and young. 'Thought she'd stop the badger digging. She did too, better than I could've done.'

'You did that on purpose?' Josh's voice was a roar.

'I was going to bring a gun and warn you off by shooting

52

over your heads. Then N – . Someone suggested I brought the bitch down. Take the dogs' minds off their jobs. Didn't know it would do it so well.' He grinned again.

'You'll burst a blood vessel, Josh Johnson. Come on in. There's beer for them as wants it, and coffee for them as don't. You won't do no more good out here tonight.' Peg's voice was sharp.

The men followed her inside, Josh coming reluctantly, urged on by the Huntsman.

'I'll teach that puppy a lesson he'll not forget,' Josh threatened, beard covered in froth.

The Huntsman downed his drink and held out his glass for a refill. Free beer was welcome as sun in the hay season.

'He's bold enough. Be fair, Josh,' he said. 'Got courage, he has, whatever you may think about him.'

'I'll lay fifty to one that Ned Foley egged him on,' Ted Wellans said irritably.

'I'll have that badger if I gas him myself,' old Tanner growled, and they turned startled heads, not knowing he was still with them. Peg, who disliked him, poured his beer with a grim mouth. The Tanners were bad farmers and worse neighbours, feckless folk whose lads went poaching on other people's land. Tanner saw her expression and grinned at her, his sunken mouth gaping, his little mean eyes admiring her tall body, crowned by a mop of unruly fair hair that had never known a hairdresser.

'Your health, missus,' he said, with a bawdy wink that made Peg itch to slap his face.

Josh, noticing her expression, decided they might just get in for a quick last drink before closing time at the *Swan*. Peg was liable to get her dander up, and then things were said that were best unspoken. And Tanner was a chancy neighbour. Those lads of his were up to all kinds of tricks.

'Peg's weary,' he said, and the Huntsman, who had also been reading the signs, stood up, easing himself awkwardly.

'I'll help her with the horses,' he said, knowing that the

three stallions were still in the field, and that, since the badger episode, Josh had insisted they were brought in for the night. 'Go and take that useless arm of yours to the *Swan* and let the poor soul have some peace.'

Peg grinned at him. She had always had a soft spot for the Huntsman, and his thoughtfulness in helping her out while Josh was out of action had endeared him even more. She began to wash the glasses while the men filed out, nodding their good nights. The Huntsman, drying up for her, listened to booted feet that tramped on the cobbles. The sounds dwindled suddenly away as the men walked on the grass verge in the narrow lane, their voices fading.

'That Tanner!' Peg said, slapping the wet cloth angrily into the water.

'Best ignored.' The Huntsman might be old, but his eyes missed little, and he summed his neighbours as shrewdly as he summed the foxes that he hunted over the years. 'A tricky man if he's thwarted.'

'Wouldn't trust him as far as the old mare can spit.' Peg was thinking of her old grey, Sally, pastured beyond the cow meadow. Sally had been pensioned off, long ago, and now led a quietly contented existence, untroubled by man or beast, with Libby the donkey for company. She shared her field with the two Shire mares. Silver, now in foal, and Pearl, who was Silver's last daughter, born the year after the Sable.

The Huntsman's thoughts had drifted away to a grey and miserable existence, in which his cottage was gone, his Siamese cat given away, Ranger belonged to another man, and he himself drowsed dully by a dismal fire, while other old men around him bickered and grumbled. Peg spoke to him twice before he answered, and then he only stared at her blankly, his expression reminding her of a stray cat that had visited her one winter evening and looked at her out of eyes so bereft that it spent the rest of its life on the farm.

'Is there something wrong?' she asked gently, her mind pondering his daughter, married and far away, the grandchildren, and the old man's health.

'Aye,' he answered sombrely. He went to the door, walking slowly, as if every bone hurt.

'Leave the horses. I'll make more coffee. Come and talk. It's not too late yet. Josh won't be back, he'll be busy clacking, cursing the botched dig with the men at the *Swan*. They often stay on after closing time, now the policeman drops in too for his pot of tea when he goes off duty.'

The Huntsman grinned. They often wondered just what was added to that pot of tea, but Mrs Jones was close-mouthed and the constable wasn't telling.

He sat back in the old wicker chair, his head dark against the brightly flowered cushion, the skin wrinkled and tanned, vivid against sparse grey hair. The tailless cat, Tinker, who had been bested by a tractor in his kitten days, jumped to his knees, purring, ecstatic, licking the man's rough coat until it was sodden. Ranger, jealous, put his head on his master's knee, and then relaxed as the rough familiar hand stroked him gently.

Peg poured coffee, and perched on a stool by the hearth, her lap an instant haven for the orange-and-white cat, Marmalade, who was shouldered jealously by Cappy, a black-and-white warrior with a mind of his own. Peg laughed, and transferred herself to Josh's roomy leather chair, scratched until the stuffing oozed, the clawing place for a lifetime filled with kittens and cats. The three settled companionably with room for all.

'Now,' she said, stirring up her cup diligently, although there was no sugar in it. 'It's better out than in.'

The Huntsman gave her one of his rare brief smiles.

'It's the Motorway,' he said. 'Right through my cottage. Sent me notice to quit.'

One of the logs in the fireplace slipped with a noise that made Peg jump. Marmie flexed his claws, startled. The fire was welcome, even on a summer night, for the big stone-floored rooms were chill, even by day, small windows keeping out the sun. Jess, lying stretched with her tummy to the blaze, twitched a hind leg in her sleep and thumped a dreaming tail. Peg found she had no words at all.

'Asked about it.' The old voice was flat, dreary with futility. Weary with fighting for an existence that he had begun to feel was not worth while. 'Nothing anyone can do. They'll give me compensation. Saw a solicitor. Just heard there's no appeal.'

Peg, suddenly feeling that coffee was inadequate, went to the cupboard for the emergency bottle of brandy and brought it out. She could still find nothing to say, but her sympathy was expressed by the gesture, for brandy at Tedder's Leigh was as rare as a swallow at Christmas.

Compensation! the Huntsman thought bitterly, savouring every drop, unable to remember when he had last tasted brandy. How could money repay the years spent on the garden, loading the soil with riches carried painstakingly from the farms, to grow roses that were prize-winners at all the local flower shows!

Years spent decorating and repairing, scrubbing and cleaning, adding a shelf here and a cupboard there, and all for nothing. Not even for the benefit of another family who would have come, bringing babies that would grow and fill the house with laughter and appreciate the time and thought that had been spent in making their home a place for pride.

The road would plunge unfeelingly through the rooms in which his wife had worked and his daughter had played, and he himself had known the laughter of childhood, the pride of manhood, and the tragedy of being left alone with only the regrets of old age. Remembering pleasures that had passed and glories that had vanished and the days when he had led a well-trained pack across the fells, all going strong, and he as vigorous as the impatient hounds and a-burst with life. . . .

'Progress!' he said bitterly to the dying blaze, and Tinker roused himself, staring with wide green eyes at the face above him, before kneading the thick cloth over the Huntsman's thigh with sudden absorbed ecstasy, purring loudly. Ranger, not to be left out, licked his master's hand.

'Have to join Jasper in the Home,' the Huntsman said. 'It's the creatures that I'll miss.'

He put down his glass and rose stiffly.

'Fretting never cured anything. And it won't bring in the horses neither. Better get on.'

He went outside, and the three stallions came at once, eager, enjoying the comfort of thick straw and the shelter of enclosing walls, and hay left in the racks beside the mangers. The mares were already indoors, in their own stable. Only old grey Sal and Libby drowsed in the dew-deep meadow.

It was good to handle the horses. To watch the dip and turn of a head, the snatch at hay, the glowing brown eyes turning trustfully to look at the man who stood beside them. He held his palm to Bruton Sable, knowing that the horse would mouth it gently, velvet lips soft against the skin, ready, as always, for human affection.

Bruton Cloud was not friendly with strangers. His affection was reserved for Josh. Warily, he watched the Huntsman ted hay into the rack, and tossed his head with displeasure when the man's hand moved towards his maned neck.

Peg, who had been locking the mares in for the night, stood for a few minutes, savouring the warm familiar horse smell, the sweep and curve of rounded quarters in each high-partitioned stall, the flicked long tails.

Outside, in the quiet of night, a last bat skidded among the trees. A cow lowed in the cattle field. The moon, light flooding behind the hills, sent radiance over byre and stable, over field and stream, and silvered the distant sparkling lake.

The Huntsman stood beside Peg, the last chore finished. He looked up, over the sweeping fells, aware of clouds of midges dancing beyond the eaves, of the first lilting call of a nightingale, hidden in the gnarled thorn in the hedge, of the glisten of petals where the dog rose bloomed, and the

57

white tangle of meadow-sweet beyond the gate.

He saluted Peg with a weary little smile and a hand half lifted, and turned back to his home, the hound walking close beside him, as if afraid that his master would vanish. Peg, watching them, found she had a lump in her throat, and, for once, as she went wearily to face the daily tussle with forms and bills on the desk, her task seemed less formidable.

CHAPTER SEVEN

JOSH, coming home late, had a wildness in him that would not allow him to seek his bed. He looked in at the stallions, each quiet in his stall. The stable was dark and friendly with the stamp and rustle and with quiet breathing.

The big, bearded man walked to the five-barred gate and leaned on it, looking at the fields, grey now, and featureless under the fading moon. An owl flew low, diving into the ditch, and he heard the small scream as a small beast died. The bird rose again, powerful wings beating slowly, and flew to rest on top of the nearest stable.

There was plenty to think about. The unpaid bills, and Peg nagging. The dead Shire, on which his hopes had been pinned. The announcement at the *Swan* that evening of a Show at Horton, where beasts could be entered to win prizes, and a sheepdog trial would be held, and Peg could go in for the cake competition and the Flower Show.

They talked of making it an institution. The Colonel's idea. There wasn't much to interest the local farm folk, not without going a long way. Appledale Show was the nearest, over fifteen miles away.

He knocked out his pipe on the gate and then faced the big thought in his head. There was to be an auction at a farm near Coniston. Old Pete Burrows had died, and all his stock was going under the hammer. House and furniture and equipment too, but it was the stock that interested Josh.

He could see the list now. Shire mare, Burrows' Sensation, in foal to Horton Steadfast King. And Steadfast King was by one of his own Shires, by Bruton Majestic himself, supreme champion at all the Shows eight, no, it must be ten years ago. He could bring back the blood of a supreme winner.

If he had the money! It was no use going to the bank. They would not increase his overdraft. He stared unhappily at the trees, black against the shadowed sky, at the cattle, quiet in the far field, at the sudden glimpse of a running fox, nose down on rabbit trails. He couldn't even hope to bid.

He went to bed, and tossed so much that Peg could have kicked him, as he heaved restlessly beside her, pumping the pillow, pulling at the covers, wishing for sleep that would not come, and that left him to rise, heavy-eyed, in the morning.

He fed the Shires, and took them out to the paddock. Another mare would be a problem. She'd have to be alone at first. Silver and Pearl might not take to her. And he didn't want her chivvied, not when she was in foal.

And once the stallions had been let to strangers, and away from one another for a few weeks, they would not settle together. He had put them in the far paddocks, separate from each other, since the fight. Half-brothers, and brought up together, so far they were amicable. But there would be trouble later, he knew from experience. Let for three months in the summer, they came back as strangers, seeming to forget the bond that once held them. Only after blistering did they seem to be able to roam together, the irritation possibly making them less aggressive towards one another.

He needed more land. Land for new paddocks. Expansion, that was what made a man rich. He strode from the field, and eyed old Sally. She could come into the near field, and the donkey with her, though goodness knew Libby would only stay where she was put if she'd a mind to.

But he'd need the new mare in the near field. Not do to leave her out of sight when she was strange and a foal coming. And he'd need to do up the old stable. Not been used for a year or so, not since he was forced to sell his three older Shires.

His thoughts fought like tomcats, so that he went in to breakfast with a headache that near blinded him, and a king-size temper. Peg set her mouth. Today there would be fireworks, non-stop. She was tired of being tactful.

She was relieved when Josh slammed the door, leaving Jess, astounded, on the wrong side of it, and the bitch whimpered as he climbed into the Land-Rover, watching him through the window, paws on the sill. The gears screeched as he bucketed out of the yard and turned sharp into the lane with a squeal of tyres that set Peg's teeth on edge and left her strung and taut, wondering if he'd killed himself or somebody else as he hammered the vehicle between the high walls and hedges.

Once on the main road, Josh settled to a steady forty, which was as much as the old rattle-trap could take. Need a new one, he thought sourly, as he turned into the field that was acting as a temporary car park, and planted it beside shining saloons and station wagons, and shabby Land-Rovers, and battered trucks. A cock glared at him malevolently from a cage in a small trailer.

The farmhouse had been old when the smugglers' packhorses brought contraband over the fells. Its small lattice-windowed rooms were dark and struck cool after the heat outside, the humid airless heat of an overcast summer day, the sky holding rain in its hummocked clouds.

The rooms were low, and many of the men stood with ducked heads, bent to avoid beam over staircase and low-lintelled doorways. Josh had to stoop more than most, and he whistled soundlessly when he saw the fixings. Done himself proud, had old Burrows, or maybe it was family stuff. Just look at that tapestry on the wall, the man's blue cloak a vivid scream of colour, an eager group congregated round it, talking excitedly and then lapsing into nonchalance, anxious not to let their interest show.

'Jacobean,' he heard a voice say, referring to the straight-backed black chairs that stood in a row near the warped door. He went outside, into the cobbled yard, where temporary pens held the bewildered cattle. Ted Wellans was looking them over, his eye on three Jersey heifers that lowed miserably in the far corner.

The mare was tied to the old bull-ring, set deep into the farmhouse wall. She was very near foaling time, and Josh sucked in his breath and stared at her, at her magnificent grey pigmentation, her beautiful stance, her massive legs, feathered, but not too much; and she turned her sad head and looked at him, and he went to stroke her – and was lost.

'Going to bid for her, then?' It was Ted Wellans, standing behind him, prosperous, lean in his dark trousers and jacket, unexpectedly seemly. 'Meeting the wife, promised to treat her to a hotel meal this evening,' he explained, aware that Josh was suddenly ill-at-ease in worn corduroys and an open-necked blue shirt. 'She's a fine mare. The knackers are here,' he added.

'The knackers!' Josh spoke hoarsely and stared at Ted. 'For a mare in foal?'

'Nobody wants a Shire these days,' Ted pointed out. He saw the expression on Josh's face. 'Look here! I'll stake you. We've been friends for long enough, Josh. It is the money, isn't it?' Everyone knew that Josh was hard put to it to make ends even look at one another let alone meet. Nowadays horses were expensive luxuries, what with the cost of feed, and shoeing, and Vet bills. Not to mention that once a man could make a fortune from his stud and let a champion stallion for a fee of one thousand guineas for twelve weeks. Now he got one hundred, if he were lucky.

Josh nodded.

'Sell the mare when she's had her foal. At the big Beast Sale. Not locally. Hear there's a friend of Jack Hinney's, Rob's American cousin, interested in Shires. Member of the American Shire Horse Society. Jack told Rob about him in a letter. Asked if there were any breeders near.'

'That mare was supreme champion last year,' Josh said. 'And she's in foal to a son of my old winner. Can't let the knackers have her.'

'I'll stake you. And you can pay me a commission if you sell her well at the Beast Sale,' Ted said, being a business man as well as a friend.

'Done.'

They formalised the pact with the farmers' handshake over a concluded bargain and went down to the *Wild Oats* to have a beer and seal it properly. The heifers and the Shire were not to be sold until after lunch.

The *Wild Oats* was soon full, of men jubilant and men downhearted. The London dealer who had bought the Jacobean chairs stood himself a double brandy and dreamed of the fancy price they would fetch when he sold them again. They were fantastic, priceless, collectors' pieces, hidden away here in this little one-horse hole, and nobody even knew what a treasure he'd got his hands on. He was a small man with smoky eyes and a thin dry manner that hid his feelings well.

Mrs Price made ham sandwiches, cutting the bread, new-baked, into thick slices, spread with creamy butter and topped with sliced home-cured ham twice as thick again. She was as lavish with mustard as with her constant teasing.

'Come on, Josh. Haven't even noticed me, and I'm big enough,' she said, her laughter as comfortable and ample as her figure. 'How's Peg?' Her round face was crumpled into a happy smile.

'Peg?' Josh, his mind full of the mare, stared at her for a moment, completely bewildered.

'He's thinking of someone else,' Mrs Price said. 'Somebody small and delicate, no doubt!'

She pirouetted on an ample leg, picked up two beermugs, and winked broadly at a tall man who had just come in, leaving the door swinging violently behind him. There was a roar of laughter.

'Matter of fact, she's even bigger than you are, Nell,' Ted Wellans said with a grin. 'Twice as big, I'd say. Come on, Josh,' he added, heaving his chair backwards, so that it scraped on the uneven well-scrubbed flags. 'Be missing those heifers.'

The yard was crowded and noisy with talk and laughter, but when the auctioneer, a nutcracker-jawed brown-faced man with a fancy way with him, went to the rostrum, which was built from two trestles that creaked ominously as he climbed up, there was a sudden hush.

The bidding started, slow at first, but livening as the better animals came into the ring. Ted got his heifers for eighty pounds a-piece and reckoned he'd done well at the price. Satisfied, he watched as they brought out the mare.

She came slowly, resisting, bewildered. Old Burrows had owned her for several years and always tended her himself. She did not like strangers and missed the affection that he had always given her. She needed a man that would understand her, and she dug in her hooves as the uncaring sales hand tried to show off her conformation and paces.

Josh swallowed and looked about him. The knackers were easy to pick out, dressed in navy suits, with bright ties and brown trilby hats, small men for the most part. One, standing near him, had wet brown eyes and a thick lipped mouth that he licked and licked again, his tongue sliding out, adder-like, every few minutes.

'Seventy guineas I'm bid. Who's offering seventy-two?'

Josh flicked his fingers. His forehead was wet with anxiety. He wanted the mare with the avidity of a child longing for its first bicycle. Eighty. Eighty-four. He swallowed as the bidding went up. He'd have to drop out. The enormity of his action suddenly overcame him and his throat went dry. What on earth would Peg say?

He heard his own voice, hoarse and unrecognisable.

'Ninety-five.'

Dear Heaven, I'm a fool.

'Ninety-eight.'

'One hundred and two.'

65

He clenched his fists, almost praying. This would have to be the last bid. He raised his hand, as if he would grab the mare from all comers. 'One hundred and five.'

'One hundred and five. Going for one hundred and five. Going for the first time.'

The hammer went down and time stopped and the world heeled. Josh's mouth was suddenly filled with saliva and he felt sick.

'Going for the second time.'

He looked at the mare. Her eyes met his. Faces blurred in front of him. Ted Wellans was solid and sober beside him, wondering if he had been wise. Suppose the upset of the auction made the mare slip her foal? Suppose. . . . He pulled himself together. A promise was a promise, and no use regretting it now. His wife would have something to say, though. He grimaced as the hammer went down for the third time.

'Gone.'

The mare belonged to Josh. He was in a dream as he watched Ted make out a cheque. He took her headrope and spoke to her gently, and she, knowing at once that here was a man who understood horses, turned trustingly and let him lead her into the shade, where he found water for her, and a patch of lush green grass to graze.

Ted went off to see to his heifers, and Josh, watching the mare, and revelling in her, thought of the problems he had to face. He had to get her home, and safely. That foal was too precious to lose. He had to keep her out of sight of the stallions, and in sight of Peg and himself so that they could watch over her. He would need space when the foal grew up. If it was a stallion it could not be put with the older Shires.

And he had to tell Peg that they were in debt for a further one hundred and five pounds. The enormity of it swamped him, until the mare reached her head towards him, asking for reassurance, and he gave it, and knew that whatever Peg might say in the first heat of the moment, this would be another forlorn beast to which she would give her heart as she always did.

For all that, he was an unhappy man as he went back to the *Wild Oats* to telephone and confess.

CHAPTER EIGHT

PEG's anger died when the mare came home. The poor
beast's head drooped, she was miserable and bewildered, she
could not understand the journey, the strangers about her,
nor the unfamiliar field into which she was put. The stallions
had been taken to the farthest field, beyond a high hawthorn
hedge, out of sight of the mares. The field was divided into
large paddocks, and each horse was alone. Josh was not
risking another fight.

The mare was miserable. Whenever Peg came into the
yard she yickered to her, looking anxiously over the gate, so
that soon Peg was behind with all the chores, as she stroked
the warm neck, spoke soothingly, and took pony nuts, held
in her hand, trying to ensure that the newcomer settled
quickly.

Later that day she heard a sudden loud bray. She had forgotten to tie the latch on the gate, and Libby, the donkey, had made her own way into her usual, but now puzzlingly forbidden, field. Anxious that the mare should not be teased, bitten, or chased, Peg ran outside, only to see the two animals rubbing noses as if they were long-lost sisters. She kept a wary eye on them, but they roamed together like life-long friends.

By now Sally, the pensioned-off mare, was mourning for the donkey, and when at last the pigs were fed, the chickens cleaned, and the churns scalded, Peg fetched the old grey from the orchard where she had been put for the time being and took her, too, into the big field, leaving the gate open behind them, and holding Sal's headrope, ready to make a hasty retreat if there was trouble.

The new Shire walked towards them cautiously, head outstretched, curious to see the mare. Peg had brought sugar lumps with her, and she held out her hand. The Shire mare nuzzled and blew wetly, took the sugar greedily, looked at old Sally, and huffed. Sally, delighted to see another of her own kind, and also happily crunching sugar, stretched her neck and rubbed her muzzle along the Shire's back. Peg removed the headrope, but remained in the field, watching.

The donkey greeted Sally with fervour. The Shire mare dropped her head and began to feed. Peg felt she could not call her Sensation. It was a ridiculous name.

'I'll call you Polly,' she decided, smoothing the sleek mane.

Josh, coming from the stallions' field, saw his wife, and grinned to himself. So Peg had come round, after all.

Peg had other ideas.

'Knacker's cheque's come,' she said.

'Good. I can pay off some of the feed bills.' Josh considered the money.

'You can bank the cheque, and the chicken money, and the money I've put by for a new winter coat, and get straight over to Wellans' and pay for that mare.' Peg's voice faltered a little, and her colour was high. 'We'll not be beholden to anyone, least of all our neighbours. You ought to be ashamed of yourself, Josh Johnson.'

'But, Peg . . .'

'Get over there, right now, or I'll go myself,' Peg said. She looked meaningly at her old bicycle, rattle-trap, sit-up-and-beg, as old-fashioned as they come, and almost as old as Ted Wellans. 'Get on now, do.'

Josh did as he was told. There'd be no peace till he'd done it. He crashed the gears irritably and the old Land-Rover coughed its way out of the yard, weary with the abuse heaped on its engine. Only five days before it had dragged a load from the fields that almost tore it apart as Josh revved and revved in an effort to get leverage.

Peg went into the house to bake the bread. She was late, and soon it would be time for milking, which she could fit in while the dough rose. She whipped up a sponge cake, made some pastry and put a pie in the oven, and then, tiring of indoors, walked over to look at the stallions.

They were peaceful enough. On one side of them, in the farthest field of all, were the milkers, placid and cud-chewing. Her handsome Friesians. In the far corner Maybelle, the bully, stood alone, the other cows giving her a wide berth. Although they had all been de-horned, Maybelle could still give little vicious kicks and butts, and make life a misery for the other cattle when she felt like it.

Don't know how they manage without de-horning, Peg thought, remembering bruises caused by Maybelle's sudden demonstrations of paddy in the milking parlour. Temperamental as they come, but for all that a fine cow and a good milker, and she had good calves, too.

In the field nearer to the house were the heifers, skittish and frisky. Mostly Friesian, but Josh had bought two Shorthorns at a sale. One of these was missing, and Peg went to look for her, anxious lest she had caught herself in wire, or fallen into the ditch. The other heifers tossed their heads, and bolted from her, unused, as the cows were, to people and handling.

There was no sign of the heifer. Puzzled, Peg came out of the field and circled it, looking for a gap. A low moo caught her ear, coming from the wrong direction. Turning her head, she saw one of the stallions, Bruton Cloud, close beside the hedge, amiably submitting to the loving ministrations of a long wet tongue, as the heifer licked him devotedly.

Peg sighed. The heifer would have to go back, and that was not going to be an easy job. Skittish and frisky, she would run all over the fields, trying to escape from the woman she was convinced meant harm to her. Josh could cope. It was time for the pie to come out of the oven, and also milking time.

She left the heifer where she was, and tramped wearily back to the farm, just in time to see the Land-Rover rock to a standstill as Josh shot through the yard gate and stamped on the brakes.

'Done it?' Peg asked.

Josh evaded the question.

'What do you think?' he enquired, a caustic bite behind the words. Peg was always getting at him. He went into the barn to get the feed ready for the horses. It would save time later. The mare needed special rations to breed a strong foal. He did not tell Peg that Ted had refused the money, gambling on a bit of commission when the beast was sold. The money was in the bank and the cheque to Ted torn up. The knowledge that he also had Peg's money added an edge to the guilt that he felt in keeping the facts from her. Ted had promised not to tell.

'Women!' Josh thought, tedding hay as if it were a personal enemy. 'Never know where you are with them. They just don't think straight.'

He ate his supper with his mind on the mare. Dai Evans had thought she was due to foal within the week. She had been pretty near, Dai knew, but old Burrows had not called him in to look at her, taking a pride himself in knowing as much as any Vet about horses.

'Think the mare might foal tonight,' Josh said abruptly, after walking out to the stable for the fifth time, leaving his supper to congeal on the plate, irritating Peg even further. Why waste time cooking for the man? she wondered morosely, toying with her own food, annoyance taking away her appetite.

'Sit down and finish your meal, man,' she said, when he stood again. 'The mare's all right. It's not her first foal, and she has them easy. Dai told you that.'

Josh took his pipe and went into the yard without answering. He stood outside the stable, listening to the mare treading the straw. She was restless, a sure sign. He glanced in at her, and she looked at him sideways, allowing him to fondle her neck, but plainly not interested in him. She had eaten her mash. That was good. He puffed contentedly, watching the swallows skim over the grass, barely six inches from the ground. More rain coming.

Peg clattered the dishes irritably in the sink. She could talk through the kitchen window.

'You moved that heifer back?' she asked.

'Aye. Took her out when I brought the stallions in. Rare old dance she led me, too, Skittish as a goat kid. Full of it.'

'You coming in?'

'I'll have coffee here. Mare's coming on. I told you.'

'Oh, you!' Peg slammed the window down, made the coffee, and took it outside. Midges were dancing in great clouds under the eaves. They never troubled Josh, but within minutes they drove her indoors again, to sit and wonder why she'd married a farmer and tied herself to a life that went on seven days a week, sometimes twenty-four hours a day.

Not had a holiday, not properly, since the boys were little lads and her brother had taken over for a few days. Now their eldest, Jack, and her brother, were both lying in graves in Malaya, and Jim was married and out in Canada with his wife and two little girls, and Dan had gone to Australia, to work on a sheep farm. Doing well, both boys, but she wished they'd write more often. She took the bread out of the oven, put it to cool on the wire tray in the pantry, and went up-stairs to bed.

As Josh walked into the stable, the mare turned her head to look at him, and then began to pull at a haybag. His own horses had racks, but the mare was used to a bag, and had looked for it, so he gave her one. She could feed without bending her head. He could not take his eyes off her. Old Burrows had known what he was about, breeding her. She was better than either of his own two mares, and suddenly he thought he would sell one of them and keep Sensation. Polly, indeed! Trust Peg.

He yawned, and went back to the house for a jersey. There was a chill in the air now that the sun had gone down. He looked over the silent fields. The cattle were dreaming, the swallows gone to roost, and in the near-dark the first bats were flittering, swooping, silent, almost shadow-like, on the insects in the air.

A small yowl startled him as Cappy laid a rat at his feet and waited for the swift praise he knew would follow. Cappy was a fine ratter, and Josh valued his services, and made sure the cat knew. Now the black-and-white warrior arched and preened himself, purring loudly. He never ate his catch. Josh took the body and buried it deep in the rose bed.

He walked back to the stable, savouring the night. There was plenty of time yet, he thought, as he glanced inside. He stiffened. The mare's head was down, her eyes intent, look-ing at something in the straw. He walked in swiftly. The foal lay beside her, wet and only an instant born. She began to lick him placidly, as he lifted his head and stared blindly at Josh, his blue eyes unfocused.

Peg must see this. At once. Josh ran up the stairs, calling

73

his wife eagerly, so that she, as he shook her wildly, woke, sure that something was wrong, and sat up, wide-eyed and terrified, expecting to hear of disaster.

'The foal's here!'

He was jubilant, eyes excited, hair on end, watching her face anxiously, and when she took in his news and hastily climbed out of the big old double bed he dashed downstairs again, knowing she would be behind him.

Peg could never resist a thing new-born. She dragged on jeans and jersey and hurried downstairs. The foal was already trying to stand. His long legs, the hooves unnaturally big, were crossed. He tried, mystified, to sort himself out while Peg grinned fondly and Josh began to bathe the mare, washing away the discomfort left by the birth. She suffered him quietly, eyes on her son.

When at last the baby was sucking, Peg brought fresh straw, and stood and fondled the mother, who gazed mildly back at her, dark eyes proud. The foal was a comfort, making up for strange people and unwelcome surroundings, but she recognised that her new owners meant well and were helping her. She stopped licking the little creature and laid her head against Peg's shoulder, her soft lips gentle.

Peg patted her and praised her and went to make warm gruel. When she brought the pan back she held it, taking pleasure in watching the mare suck greedily, not missing a single drop.

'Spend the night downstairs, watching her,' Josh said gruffly. 'Can't have anything go wrong now.'

Peg nodded. This was routine.

'It's a good job you paid Ted back,' she said absently, as the foal turned and flickered his ears at the sound of her voice. He had no fear of people. These, present so soon after his birth, were an instantly accepted part of his new astonishing world, like his mother. He did not even flinch as Peg laid a hand on his grey pelt.

'Just like Polly. He's a beauty!' Peg was enthusiastic.

His sire had been grey, too. He would be another Steadfast King.

'Why is it a good job we paid Ted?' Josh asked, with a sinking heart.

'We can't sell her. You know that. Look at that foal. Think what would happen if we bred her with the Cloud, or even with Sable. Now, that foal would be a sensation. They're both better Shires than Horton Steadfast King. Better than Burton Majestic. You know that.'

'Peg, Peg!' Josh said, exasperated. One minute on him for buying the mare at all, the next black-determined not to part with her.

'We haven't got room.' Josh rubbed his hand through his thatched red hair.

'We can manage. Just one mare. Won't make all that difference.'

'And the foal?' Josh asked. 'We must sell him.'

'We'll show him first and get a better price,' Peg answered, her eyes dreamy as she surveyed her future champion. 'We'll call him . . . ' She paused.

'Best name him Bruton Hope,' Josh said. 'Make our fortune for us yet, maybe.'

'You'll keep them?' Peg's voice was eager.

'Go to bed, old girl. The next foal will be called Rare Sensation.' He grinned at her, his expression mocking.

'You're an old fool, Josh,' Peg smiled at him, her eyes suddenly gentle. 'We're both old fools.'

She gave a backward look at the foal, now settling to sleep, the mare beside him. Josh had forgotten her, absorbed in a final check on mother and son, and knowing that very soon he would have to face Ted, and this time insist he took the money. He couldn't sell either beast. He couldn't bear the thought of parting with Sensation, who had already shown her gentle nature. And her breeding was superb. He'd have to match her with a grey. He sighed contentedly. She was a wonderful brood mare. It was good to have a grey stallion coming up again among the blacks. He and the Cloud would make a pair.

He settled to dreaming, while Cappy, breathless with anticipation, crouched, eager-eyed, waiting for a mouse to come out of a hole on the other side of the cobbled yard. Marmalade sat in the moonlight and washed, and Tinker, who adored horses, came to see what his master was doing so late at night, and curled up beside the mare in the straw, his eyes, bright with interest, watching the foal.

The cat's ears moved backwards, alert, whenever the little beast snuffled, which was often. The mare did not mind the cat. Old Burrows had had twelve of them, and often two or three kept her company, at night, sometimes curling to sleep in the manger, while the kittens played in the straw beneath her feet.

Peg, lying listening to the calling owl, the eerie yelp of the badger, going for water in the spilling brook, brimful from heavy summer rain that had fallen on the hills, thought of the foal with wonder. She could never be indifferent to the new young animals born on the farm. Each one was a small miracle, and she wished that they need not grow up.

It would be good to watch the new baby find his feet, play in the fields, investigate bracken and heather and buttercup, all parts of the astonishing world that had just been given him.

The thought of the bills nagged at the back of her mind, but for once did not dominate her. Something would turn up. They weren't broke yet, not by a long chalk. It was just the constant juggling that got her down. Not like having a salary paid regularly month by month. And animals needed feeding, all the time.

She drifted into a dream which Josh matched, waking. Seeing his new foal carry off every honour there was, at every Show in the country. He did not think of fees and the cost of carrying the beasts. Life was suddenly perfect. He went outside to smoke his pipe, and watched dawn lighten the sky, heard the first clear call of a bird, followed by waves of sound that trilled from every coppice and bush, louder and louder, until the world was as wide awake as the cockerel that added his raucous welcome to the dawn.

High on the hill, ears cocked, Ruff heard the chorus, and made his way stealthily towards Tanner's farm. He passed the badger, but did not scent him, and Old Brock grunted and turned aside, full after a night's hunting, and not eager to fight. He came home in the moments between cockcrow and the first flooding light from the sun climbing the sky, and Josh, seeing him, frowned. He'd get that old beast yet, and have no more damage done to his horses.

CHAPTER NINE

HORTON SHOW ceased to be a project on paper, and became a reality. Committees met and wrangled and bickered and fought. Life-long friends became bitter enemies as ideas were torn to pieces, put aside, and shelved. Slowly, out of the welter of irritation, arrangements began to be made.

Nobody in the village had organised a Show before. It was soon evident that no one knew how to begin, and the Colonel, hearing of troubles in plenty, offered a hand, and brought in three people who had experience of other Shows.

Resentment smouldered. Why should strangers run the Horton Show? But at last their worth was recognised. The committee members realised that hard work must be done, and soon the villagers from Horton and Buttonskille, from Burnet and Bruton-under-the-Water, were eagerly entering

78

for flower show and dog show, for beast show and cake competition, while mothers stitched frantically at fancy dresses, children collected wild flowers for their own flower class, and small girls on ponies jumped perilously over small obstacles, practising desperately for the gymkhana.

'Whole place 'as gone mad,' said Bess Logan sourly after waiting near on twenty minutes in the post office to buy half a pound of tea, while the women in front of her discussed anxiously the possibility of putting those who made cakes with electric mixers into a different class from those who mixed them by hand.

'Not fair, else,' said Rosie Needler, a neat, pert, pretty woman who prided herself on her baking, but had no money to spare for expensive gadgets to ease her day's work.

'Nothing's fair in this life,' Bess said tartly, anxious to get home, where too many chores waited her. Not got the strength she used to have, and too slow, and it took so much more time to walk to the village these days, and her rheumatism never eased, not even in summer.

The older women made way for her, uneasy in her presence, remembering that her great-grandmother had been burned as a witch, and there were those that said that Bess herself had the evil eye. Not that any of them were superstitious, in these days of the telly, and of fast motor cars that were more like black magic than anything that old Annie Logan dreamed up; but it never did any harm to be careful.

Josh, reading that there was a class for Shire horses, and that five other men, old rivals of his, were entering theirs, thought deeply and finally decided to show the Bruton Cloud. He was the best and easiest of the three. Least likely to be nervous in crowds. The Sable was unpredictable, and Bruton Ebony had torn his shoulder, leaning over barbed wire, in an attempt to get at the lusher grass in the verge beyond the field.

He went to look at the stallions and clucked with annoyance. The heifer was back, standing beside Bruton Cloud as if she were a horse, and not a cow. She had broken through the hedge this time. He could see the gap. Lucky none of the others had followed her. There was little enough grass on the thin soil as it was. A herd of heifers would take all the grazing.

He went to head her off, back to her own field, but she'd have none of him, and raced around. He was irritable and breathless. Then, quite suddenly, she was meek as maybe, and went back to join her sisters. He found enough dead wood to fill the gap and pulled it into the hedge.

He was halfway across the cowfield, going home for tea, when the Cloud whinnied a greeting, and turning, he saw the gate standing wide, and the heifer back with the stallion. He went over and examined the latch. She had lifted it with her nose, determined to have her own way. Having unlatched the gate, the Cloud had pushed it open. He seemed to be glad of her company.

Josh closed the gate again, leaving her with the Shire. The horse seemed to want her, and she was so tricky that she would do any amount of damage to gain her own end.

That night, when he brought the horses in, he began to groom the Cloud, giving him extra time to ensure that his coat gleamed, and mane and tail shone sleek and splendid, like spun silk. He added cod-liver oil to the bran, and whistled as he spread fresh bedding for the mares.

Excitement seethed and smouldered. Jasper put polythene bags over his roses, to keep the wet from them. The Huntsman was entering Ranger for the obedience trial, and took him daily into the fells, where he often met Ned Foley, restless with summer, unable to confine himself to the house.

Ted Wellans looked at his animals and decided to put his best milker in for the dairy class. Sheba was a fine Jersey, with every chance of being a winner. He watched over her, and he gave his wife advice as she practised her cake making, and supervised his daughters, putting their horses to jumps that Rob Hinney made for them out of stakes and furze bushes. No pony dragged a leg over those prickles after the first time.

Eyes watched the sky constantly, trying to predict the weather. They needed a fine day, and plenty of people. Expenses had mounted unbelievably. The catering alone cost a small fortune, and nothing ambitious at that. Scones and cakes, made by volunteers, and sandwiches from the bakery, hot dogs for the lads. The Scouts were taking care of those, holding a barbecue. Tea, ice-cream, and lemonade. Yet how the bills mounted!

Bills for posters, which were badly smudged and had to be done a second time. Bills for programmes, which failed to turn up, and finally appeared at the eleventh hour with the wrong date on them and were altered painstakingly by hand by a committee of people foaming over other people's incompetence.

Bills for balloons, and hydrogen to fill them, to send them on a long-distance competition; bills for the hire of marquees, and the hire of the field which the farmer refused to have ruined for nothing; for pens for the stock, and for teacups and saucers.

Benches and tables were borrowed from the school and the Sunday school, and Mick Stacy suddenly endeared himself to everybody by organising the older boys into a fool-proof team of messengers that coped with emergencies, and fetched the Colonel, or the Vicar, or the local builder, a willing assistant, or the Scoutmaster to deal with the latest mishap.

Jack Hinney, Rob's cousin from America, turning up in the middle of the turmoil with his family, come on holiday, was mightily amused. He threw himself vigorously into the preparations, offering to help blow up the balloons, lending his wife – rather to her irritation – to the Ladies' Committee, admiring the flowers treasured in the gardens, and Jasper's roses, bonneted like milkmaids to keep out the wet. His great good humour helped enormously to smooth out woes, and it was easier to bestbehave in front of a comparative stranger.

'Kids want to see a Hunt,' he said, leaning on the rough wall one morning just before the Show, as the Huntsman drilled his own hound. Ranger was co-operative, but there were hares on the hill, and the scent of fox and rabbit lay strong on the grass. He felt as itchy as a boy in school on a midsummer afternoon when the trout were lying in pools for the taking and thoughts of cool water, perfect for swimming, were more insistent than the schoolman's drone.

'A Hunt? But you don't hunt in summer!'

The Huntsman was as shocked as if Jack had committed blasphemy.

The American's bright eyes stared.

'No hunting in summer?' He couldn't believe it, and disappointment was bitter. All this way, and the kids wouldn't even see the very thing he'd brought them for.

'Cubbing starts in September.' The Huntsman flicked his fingers, and Ranger sat, watching him, though his eyes strayed constantly to the rough clumps of heather and tussocky grass, and the rocky fell in plain sight up the hill, where, even now, a brown hare went bounding.

'Can't stay till then,' Jack said glumly. 'Thought it would be quite a sight for the kids. Something they'd remember all their lives. They might never come to Europe again.'

The Huntsman considered Europe with a small start of surprise. Fiercely insular, it had never occurred to him that other people might consider England part of a larger continent, and not the firm island entity that he knew.

'Tell you what,' he said at last. 'We can put on a hound trail.'

'How do you do that?' Jack swung himself on to the wall, and started guiltily as one of the top stones slipped into the ditch with a small crash and a ferment of dust. He got down again and carefully fitted it back into place. 'Forgot your walls are loose,' he explained, a mite sheepish.

'So do lots of folk,' the Huntsman reassured him, anxious to be polite to a visitor from overseas. He looked at Ranger.

'Right, lad, but back you come when you're called,' he said cheerfully, the fine weather and company having driven off for the time being the knowledge that his home was soon to vanish and that his own future was bitterly uncertain.

The hound bounded away, the sun gleaming on his well-groomed coat, mouth open, tongue lolling, long ears flapping as he ran. There were too many enticing smells for serious hunting, and he was teased by a fresh evocative scent from every heather tump, so that he cast from one to the other like a pup, never concentrating, too full of summer and happiness at being free to work seriously.

'Tom fool pup,' the Huntsman said affectionately, his little leathery face crinkling with entertainment. He gave his mind to more important things.

'You drag a scent on the trail you want the hounds to work,' he said. 'Might be a dead fox in a sack, or aniseed, or rank meat in a sack. Do it before you take the pack out.' He nodded thanks for Jack's well-filled tobacco pouch and busied himself with his pipe. 'Pack's not been worked since hunting ended. They'll be raw.'

'Kids won't know that,' Jack said. He had three of them, a trio of pretty daughters of whom he was vastly proud. Shelley, the eldest, going on seventeen, was horse-crazy, fourteen-year-old Sallie was the one for a dog, a queer little tomboy with a wildly affectionate way with her; Cherry, the ten-year-old, was the quiet one, always reading.

'I'll work on them. Tell the men in the *Swan* tonight. We're meeting to talk about the last arrangements for the Show. Scouts've asked for a pet show, on top of everything, and schoolmaster thinks it's good idea. Means more entry fees.'

'Pets? Cats and dogs?' Jack Hinney asked, his eyes following Ranger, who was circling above him on the hill, nose down to some trail that seemed worth following.

'That's the trouble,' the Huntsman answered. He puffed contemplatively, enjoying the rare blue sky above him, the mirrored lake lying below, patched with white flecks where the wind played friskily on the water, the brilliant greens of the trees that would soon fade to drabber midsummer hues. 'Youngest lad of Rob Hinney's got a grass snake, one of the Tanner boys has three hedgehogs. There's rabbits and hamsters and guinea-pigs, and a fox Ned Foley found orphaned after a Hunt two years since, and gave to little Jeannie Lee. See that among the dogs and cats!'

'Have to borrow cages,' Jack Hinney said. 'Should be enough in a farming area. Can't let the kids down. Besides, mine'd like to see a pet show, like that. Wonder if your grass snake is the same as ours?'

'This one's called George, and Tommy wears it half the time. Schoolmaster gets mad as it goes to school and gets loose and all the girls start screaming!'

Jack Hinney laughed.

'Never a dull moment. You'll fix a trail for me, then? Be an attraction for the Show, if you run it during the afternoon, you know. Advertise it, and you'll have every American in the Lakes over to watch.'

'Bit late to advertise it,' the Huntsman said, whistling. Ranger came running, tired of his play. He dropped at his master's feet and looked up with such wise eyes and worried wrinkled face that Jack Hinney laughed.

'Cares of the world on his shoulders, poor old lad,' he said, and the dog's long stern beat joyously on the hard ground, making a bird in a nearby straggling thorny bush scold in anger.

'Leave the advertising to me,' Jack said, enormously pleased at being able to help. He had fallen hard for Bruton-under-the-Water, feeling that his kinship with Rob Hinney brought him very close to the villagers and made him one of them.

The Huntsman nodded to him, and went off to find the owners of the hounds, and arrange for them to be brought to him for drilling. His mind went over them. Bella, Painter,

Flier, Madam, Ranger, Swiftsure. Three couples. Maybe he could drill four, but there was so little time.

So little time. Jasper, cherishing his roses, stared glumly at them. His last year in the garden where his hands had brought beauty to life. He treasured his flowers, although there was room for very few. His rough hands stroked a giant Peace, flushed with high summer.

Nell watched him, anxious, sensing more and more a fear in him that was borne through to her, so that she followed him everywhere, desperate lest he vanished as her first master had done. He had gone to jail for ten years when the red setter bitch was eight years old. Jasper had taken her in when his old terrier, Skim, was killed by a badger, when rescuing Bella and Madam from an underground tunnel where they had been trapped while hunting a fox on their own.

So little time. Josh, guarding the Cloud, gentling him, grooming him, polishing the harness till it gleamed, thought of the Jet and sighed. He'd been a surefire winner. The Cloud was young, not yet come to glory. He needed to fill out.

Tedding hay, bringing feed, fixing the cows in the milking parlour, Josh's thoughts turned more and more to his rivals, pondering the likelihood of too much competition.

The three brewery stallions. Betwick's Major, Betwick's Brigadier, and Betwick's General. Now those were horses! Coal-black, every last one of them, all with three white socks, and with enough cups and prizes and certificates and rosettes to fill a small room. Betwick's groom, Tim Malcolm, knew all there was to know.

'Stop glooming and come and help me, for goodness' sake,' Peg said, exasperated, two nights before the Show. She was white-washing the barn at the far end of the farm, watching with absorbed interest by the three cats, a speckled hen, and the old rooster.

Josh joined her, work being as good a cure for worry as anything else he knew, but his eyes went back to the Shire,

85

and he put him in the stable early, afraid that the badger might take a sudden urge upon him to come out and put paid to yet another chance of success.

CHAPTER TEN

THE day of the Show dawned fine but blustery. Clouds like rabbit-scuts skidded, dancing, across a speedwell sky. The wind had a way with it, tossing paper, blowing hats, teasing the corners of the big marquee, and the edges of the girls' skirts, streaming the bunting, and chasing the dust.

The Huntsman looked out of his window, frowning. The hounds would be wind-crazed, edgy and irritable, possibly unbiddable after several weeks without discipline. If only he could run a proper pack. He wondered whether to take them out for a trial early run, and decided against it.

Josh cursed vigorously. Horses hated breeze and bluster, and the Cloud was no exception. Stand him in the judging ring, and if the judge was in the wrong place, as well he might be in an amateur-run Show, the Shire would try to turn his tail into the wind, and refuse to stand. He'd edge away when he was showing his paces. The prize would go to a more biddable and patient horse.

The badger, running home in the late aftermath of dawn, also wind-bothered, yelped as he went to his sett, and Josh saw his wide rump vanish, and swore. A symbol of bad luck. He might as well stay at home for the good it would do him. They must have another dig. Get the brute out once and for all. He felt an unreasonable animosity towards it.

He had more than enough to do, as Peg was helping with the teas, and had gone early to butter scones and cut bread, and lay tables. He did her chores as well as his own, checked on the mares and the foal and the stallions, and then came to ready the Cloud for the Show.

The Cloud had never been braided before. He shook his head irritably, trying to free his mane from the confining ribbons and gay standards. He wanted none of it. Once he brought his head round angrily, catching Josh on the chin and making him swear. Once he kicked out against the edge of the stall, not to hurt his master, but to show his displeasure.

It was hot in the stable, but when Josh took the Shire into the yard the wind irritated the big horse. He turned him tail into it, but then the tail proved awkward to fix, and three times the Cloud swished it out of his hand, jerking away nervously.

It took longer than Josh had expected, and when, himself dressed in his Sunday best, and the farm locked up, and the other animals safe, he led the Cloud out into the lane, he found himself with a pack of trouble on his hands.

They had to head into the wind all the way. The horse twisted, hating the feel of moving invisible air on his face, and the dust that eddied and swirled. He was not used to traffic. A car, passing too fast, too close, and stupidly accelerating with a whine of gears, sent him into the hedge, trembling, hooves planted firm, refusing to move.

Wellans' new horse, Black Diamond, bought only a few weeks ago for the girls to ride, and not yet ready for road work, came galloping behind a hedge to look at the enormous creature plodding outside, and so frightened the Shire that he pulled to the far side of the road, almost dragging Josh off his feet.

Josh paused to catch his breath and wonder if he ought to go home. As usual, he had not stopped to consider before bringing the Shire along an unfamiliar road. But if he was going to show the Cloud he had to get used to people and crowds and other animals. He should have put him in the horse box, but it hadn't seemed worth it, not for the sake of a quarter of a mile. By the time they reached the gates of the big field, Josh was exhausted and his patience was wearing thin.

The Cloud looked at the crowds warily. His sensitive ears flicked ceaselessly, picking up weird and unfamiliar sounds. Josh prayed that no child with a balloon would come near. He had never been so thankful in his life as he was when they reached the big paddock set aside for the Shires, and was able to put his own in a temporary enclosure, and accept gratefully the long cool drink of lemonade that Peg sent him. He thanked the child that brought it and lit his pipe, leaning on the railing, summing up his rivals as he did so. There was an hour before the class judging.

The bulk of the crowd was outside on the fells where the Huntsman had four couples of hounds waiting to start. Jo Needler, grinning, was bookie, collecting bets from the owners, and Jamie Leigh, a delighted grin on his face, and a little too much beer in his stomach, called the odds.

Down in a far corner of the field Mick Stacy was coping with a far bigger entry of pets than he had expected. Boys had been sent hastily to borrow cages, a cat had escaped and run home, its small owner following it, sobbing bitterly. Two dogs had bitten each other, and Dai had rendered hasty first aid, and advocated permanent separation on far sides of the enclosure.

Mick, hotter than he had expected, and bothered by the restlessness of the animals, due, though he did not realise it, to the wind, tried to keep the children from quarrelling as bitterly as the dogs.

Pete, the youngest Tanner boy, hot and sticky in his Sunday school outfit, wandered among the cages, ripe for mischief. He thought the Show was daft. He thought his mum was daft, dressing him up in his best, grey-trousered and hot, and he thought schoolmaster daft too. Always on about something.

The Huntsman flicked his fingers. Pete Tanner, looking across the field, saw Swiftsure leap into a flying start, followed by Painter, and a moment later, he glanced at the cage beside him, and saw Jeannie Lee's pet fox. Jeannie was a mite simple, and it was fun to tease her. He opened the cage door.

Foxy was as hot and cross as the rest of them. He was a young dogfox, and he lived with the Lees, in the house, having the distinct conviction that he was a dog. He played with the dogs and fed with them, and as he refused to come when he was called, Jeannie coupled him with a small chain to the old sheepdog when she took the animals out. When she called Bitty, the fox had to come too.

Foxy had never seen such a crowd, and he did not like it. The schoolmaster, his eyes on a pair of small boys ready to come to blows over the respective merits of their own dogs, did not see Foxy ease himself on half-bent legs and slip away.

People standing near, watching the hounds, only half-looked, and did not realise at once that they were seeing a fox, and not a dog looking for fun among the crowd. Foxy was free.

He was not sure that he liked the sensation. He had never known it before. His mother had been killed when he was still a tiny cub, unweaned, and Ned had found him and brought him to meat-eating stage, and then given him to Jeannie.

He had never been shown the ways of the hill, the safe trails to take him from the hounds, the places in which he might hide, the earths and setts and holes in rock, the ditches and drains and tunnels and becks that would mask his scent and carry a wild beast to safety.

He wanted Jeannie, but she was not to be seen, so he turned, seeking cover, and crept into the ditch where he sheltered for some time. Unluckily, he was sitting on the hound trail and a few minutes later Painter burst through the hedge bottom, caught his scent, and bayed eagerly.

Foxy did not know about hounds, but instinct stood him in good stead and he bolted along the hedge bottom, the pack on his heels. The Huntsman, seeing his brush, and bewildered by the presence of the fox among people, tried to call them off. It was not the hunting season in any case, and he had an uneasy feeling someone could prosecute him.

The hounds did not care. They had quarry in sight and no amount of calling would head them now, much to Jack Hinney's disappointment. He had just been telling his daughters how very obedient they were.

Foxy, aware that he could not head his pursuers off, or out-distance them, decided the best thing was to face the devil he knew and go to people. He had always known kindness from people, and he might find Jeannie, or her father yet.

Jeannie, coming away from the ice-cream cart, saw his brush, and screamed. She ran towards the fox, blundering into staring folk who thought the child had gone crazy. Mick Stacy, turning and seeing the empty cage, hearing the yelling pack, seeing the Huntsman run like a demented creature, bounded over the rail and out of the pet enclosure, running swiftly towards the hounds.

People, realising suddenly that this was a fox and not a

dog, moved out of the way. Some of the visiting women cried out, as the scared beast hurtled among them, mouth panic-open, eyes wide and terrified. It was much worse for a petted beast to become sudden prey.

Painter was catching up. Swiftsure turned, almost bringing down a man watching the Shires. He fled along the edge of the field, jaws open and tongue lolling, eyes bright and mischievous. Pete Tanner, suddenly dismayed as he saw Madam bowl into a table full of glasses and send it flying, slipped away through a back entrance.

'Foxy! Foxy!'

Jeannie was almost hoarse with shouting, but the fox was too frightened to hear. He chased on, dashing into a sanctuary that proved short-lived, for it was the tea tent, and women shrieked so that he slipped out of the other side, and found himself on the outside edge of the Shire field.

The field was open and empty. The Shires were standing, silent, waiting their turn, each one with a man beside him. The men were anxious. The noise and shouts and screams were upsetting the big horses so that they moved restlessly. The Cloud had flattened his ears, a sign that made Josh tighten his mouth, and stand alert, ready for trouble.

Foxy streaked under the rail. Jeannie, at the far end of the field, called to him, and her father, hearing her, came running, and stared, horrified, as Painter flung himself forward and romped across the open field, only a few yards behind the other animal.

Mick Stacy, watching the line the fox was taking, made for the car park. With any luck, the poor brute would end up there, and he might be able to do something, though what, he didn't know. Pete Tanner would rue this bitterly, he thought angrily, immediately certain of the culprit. The schoolmaster could not bear any beast being hunted, or killed.

The fox came so close to Josh that the Cloud reared. He

twisted, angrily, disliking dogs almost as much as the Jet had done, his ears flat, ready to trample the creature in front of him, Josh gripped him hard and spoke soothingly, using words that meant little, but that always gentled his beasts. The Cloud quietened, but Josh was not happy about him, sensing that there was something more wrong than dislike of the racing fox.

There was a yell from the car park.

The fox, feeling the hunters close behind him, had run among the cars. These were familiar, for he often rode in the Lees' old Land-Rover, coupled to Bitty.

Mick, with a flash of insight that baffled him when he thought about it afterwards, raced to the Lees' shabby old vehicle, climbed in, opened the front passenger door, and, the keys being in the ignition, turned on the engine, racing it, hoping for the best.

Foxy knew that engine. He heard it, a familiar sound, close at hand, and skidded on his tracks, turning until he found the vehicle that was part of home. He leaped inside, and crouched on the floor trembling, while the schoolmaster slammed the door.

Outside the car the hounds bayed, furious and frustrated. The Huntsman came to them, angry and humiliated and gave them the rough side of his tongue. They cowered and turned, hangdog, tail-down, abject, and went back with him on to the fells.

The Huntsman sent them off on the trail, but they were tired and dejected, the crowd had had more fun than it had bargained for, and wanted tea and ice-cream and a bit of enjoyment, and he called them off, disappointed, while Jo Needler and Jamie Leigh gave the money back to those who had made bets, and cursed the fox.

Only Jack Hinney was content, for contrary to all expectations, his daughters had seen a real Hunt. They had seen the fox run for cover, and the hounds on the trail, and would have something to tell their class-mates when they went back to school.

Rob Lee went across to his Land-Rover, his arm round Jeannie, who was his youngest and his pet, and who, with her half-simple ways, needed more loving than most lasses. He found Mick Stacy sitting with the fox crouched against him, slowly relaxing as a warm gentle human hand coaxed and stroked him.

Rob opened the door.

'Foxy!' Jeannie held out her arms.

The little beast greeted her like a boisterous dog, jumping at her, snuggling into her arms, licking her face, unbelievably content to be safe and with his mistress again.

'You stay here with him, love,' her father said. 'You'll be O.K.?'

She nodded trustingly.

'All safe now, Jeannie,' Mick Stacy said gently, and Jeannie looked up at him dumbly, her eyes wide. She liked this schoolmaster who was never cross with her, but spent long hours explaining to her just what the strange things at school really meant. Soon she would be able to read, like the others, he said, and she knew he meant it.

'I'd best get back and see what the other little devils are up to.' He yawned as he followed Rob Lee among the crowded cars.

Rob held out his hand.

'Thanks, mister,' he said, and that was all, but the warm smile and friendliness in his eyes told Mick Stacy that now at least one man had accepted him. Perhaps others would follow suit. He felt happier than he had for weeks as he went back to judge the pets and found Jack Hinney and his three daughters doing that for him.

'You've got to live here afterwards,' Jack said with a broad grin. 'Better let a stranger do it.'

The schoolmaster, going over to the tea tent for a drink, stopped to look at the Shires. All beauties. He knew Josh's

94

but had never seen them in such numbers before. The Cloud was the sleekest, but even Mick Stacy's inexpert eye could see that he had not the magnificent presence of the three brewery horses, who were much older beasts.

The judge nodded, his face impassive, as a farmer from the other side of Horton Mere led out his mare, a splendid docile patient grey. She walked regally, trotted nobly, stood quietly, and at the end walked off with immense dignity.

It was Josh's turn.

The Cloud was uncomfortable. Nerves had upset him, and pain had been needling him off and on all day. The wind was maddening him. He was facing into it, as Josh had feared, and although aware that he must be quiet, he was desperate to turn his tail. He took five paces forward, Josh proud beside him, and then the niggling ache that had been present ever since he had had to stand still for the motor car, knifed into violent life.

He gave a shrill yicker, and rolled.

Josh jumped out of the way, his face suddenly white. He pulled at the headrope.

'Up boy, steady now. Come, boy. Good boy.'

The Cloud was on his feet again. There was a sigh from the crowd. The judge nodded, eyeing the horse with interest. He was young and would improve. He was going to be a winner. A beauty. Perfect. Head, shoulders, stance. Lovely.

The Cloud rolled again, this time pain filling his mind with fear. His hooves flailed the air.

Dai ran forward.

Josh stood mutely as the Vet looked at the horse, who had struggled to his feet again.

'It's colic, Josh. Sorry, he'll have to be disqualified as unfit. Don't think it's a bad attack. Possibly nerves. Keep him walking. I'll look in on my way home.'

Sadly, Josh began to walk the Shire off the field. The big horse plodded beside him, the agony easing a little as he moved. The judge, compassionate, walked over to commiserate.

'He's a fine horse. It's bad luck, but he'll be a winner in a year or two. Mark my words.'

It was small consolation.

As Josh walked the Cloud slowly homewards down the sunlit lane he remembered his glimpse of the badger that morning.

'Said that damned beast was bad luck,' he announced to a bird preening itself in a hedge. The bird flew away.

CHAPTER ELEVEN

THE *Swan* was quiet of nights. The Huntsman, bitterly disappointed by his last drag, and more and more aware of the shortness of time left to him before the new motorway knifed through the cottage and left him homeless, stayed alone, glooming into the empty hearth.

Jasper, too, had no heart for company. He was old and nobody wanted him, an old nuisance in the chimney corner, old gaffer, ripe for a pint and a spot of reminiscence when summer visitors came, and off they'd go and laugh behind his back. A figure of fun; an old fool; no wonder they wanted to put him in a Home.

Milking the cows, conscious all the time of their reassuring warmth, of their soft sweet breath, of the rich creamy liquid foaming into the bucket, ready for himself and Bess Logan and the Huntsman, and one or two of the other villagers, he became surly and irritable.

Patient with the animals, he was short with people, sparing no time for more than a curt dip of his head. The sight of the doctor, in his shining big car, busy on his rounds, or the District Nurse, in her little runabout, made him turn away. When they were out of sight he would stare after them, hating their security and arrogance, resentful of their youth. They were responsible for his plight, declaring him too old to live alone.

Most of the men were too busy to be more than half aware of the change in the Huntsman and the old farmer. Only Ned Foley, temporarily resting from some of his summer casual jobs, and sensitive as an animal to other folks' feelings, knew of the malaise that troubled them, and visited them both, but was unable even to stir the mists of despondency that seemed to have settled over them.

Jasper, perhaps, was in the better case. He could not leave his cows and chickens, and he pottered around his scrap of land, and fed his roses, even though he knew they would soon be dug up. He could not bear to neglect them, and work prevented too much brooding.

The Huntsman had no incentives left. Why walk out on the fells and look for fox trails, note the new earths, or take the hounds for exercise? Another man would run the pack next year, if another could be found to take it on for pleasure and no fee, and that he doubted. Few men in England now wanted the bother, or even had the time to take the hounds and drill them until they formed a pack. Ned, talking of a hen-killer up above Buttonskille, met with no luck. He might have been talking about the price of tea, or a lost penny, for all the Huntsman knew or cared.

Even in the *Swan*, trying to interest the other men, Ned knew failure. Mrs Jones was struggling with a bad back, her mind on the pain that dominated so much of her day and night, wondering if she would, as the doctor said, have to lie up for a few weeks, and if so, who would take on, and what would happen to her licence. If the brewery had to replace her, she might not get her job back again.

Josh, surly with disappointment, brooded into his beer-mug, his red beard sparkling with spilled droplets. The badger was becoming an obsession, his wits against those of a wild beast that lived on his land and plagued him. It angered Peg, who thought him absurd, but there was no arguing once his mind was made up.

Ted Wellans, who had started in good faith to find fresh accommodationn for Jasper, had bumped his head in turn against the local council, and the town council, and the County Council, against landlords, and against the welfare authorities, who maintained that it was absurd for a man as old as Jasper to live alone. Anything might happen to him, and his beasts would suffer.

No use telling them that in a village no man was ever alone. Bess Logan, cackle-headed and sour-minded though she was, would no more dream of letting a day pass without checking on the old farmer, just to make sure he was out and about, than she would have dreamed of attending a garden party.

If Jasper failed to bring the milk there were at least five women who would go and see what ailed him, aye, and stay and help, tidying up and taking care of the beasts, and see-ing that the old man was fed. No use telling that to townfolk. They looked at you, chill-eyed and not understanding. There a man could die and lie for a week, and his neighbours not bother. Not intruding, they called it. Ted had another name for it.

He did not know where next to start, and the news that the Huntsman also was to go was bitter. Who would take over the pack, and train it? Who would lead the Hunt for them? They had to keep down the foxes, and hounds were surer than guns. At least you knew, if there was a kill, that it was quick, and you had not left a beast to run with a festering bullet in its body that would kill it by torture over long suffering weeks.

'Any joy, Ted?' Ned Foley's small wrinkled face was anxious; he had a feeling for men as well as beasts, and it was not right that at the end of his days a man should be flung out of the place that he'd been raised in.

Ted shook his head, eyes unhappy. He had a new dog beside him, Tello, a young Labrador, full of vitality, but still foolish with youth, that sat sloppily against his leg, body slumped, head on knee, eyes adoring.

'Tried everything.' Ted thumped his hand on the table, making Painter bark and Jo Needler jump and spill his beer and swear. 'It's a damned shame. Pack of bureaucrats up there.'

It sounded to Mrs Jones as if he was referring to a hypothetical heaven rather than the County town.

'They can boss us and tell us where to go and what to do, and we're as helpless as my cattle when I sell them off to the butcher. It's not right.'

'Must be sommat we can do.' Rob Lee was a slow-speaking man, who took a long time to make up his mind to speak at all. 'Be like my Jeannie. They wanted to take her away from us, and put her in a special school. We wouldn't have it, and in the end we stuck out, and she's come on a treat at home.'

'There's nothing much wrong with Jeannie,' the schoolmaster said, from his half-hidden stool in the corner. He pushed a hand through his blond hair, a puckish-looking man with wise eyes that belied his years. He'd had a rough childhood. It had not made him tough, but had, instead, given him a vast sympathy for the under-privileged. 'She's a bit slow, but she's a perfectly normal child. The teasing the others have always given her has frightened her wits away. I've stopped that.'

He did not add that he gathered from the children's behaviour that their previous schoolmaster had been a sadistic man with a bitter tongue, and a ready cane, enough to frighten a normal child, let alone a sensitive one like Jeannie; but that the villagers knew from experience. A warmth of feeling for Mick Stacy lightened the atmosphere. He might be odd with his views on hunting, but at least he was honest, and the kids liked him, and that proved a lot.

'Have one on me,' Ted Wellans said, and Mick accepted with a smile, the tenseness draining from him, so that, relaxed and friendly, the men found him much more likeable and easy.

'Perhaps I can help with your problem,' he said, taking his glass from Ted. 'I've more free time than you, and we've two weeks break at Whit. I can find out how the land lies. . . . Maybe get up a signed petition.'

'You can try,' Ted said wearily. 'Thought I had a pull with the County Council, and through the Agricultural people. Like trying to kill a pheasant with a pin. Makes you sick.'

He tossed his drink off, and went out, anxious to look at Sheba, who had won first prize for the best milker at the Show, but who was showing signs of being off her food. He was uneasy about her, and Rob Hinney, looking her over only that morning, had shaken his head.

'Don't like it. Don't like it at all,' he grumbled. And it wasn't like Rob to get the wind up.

The door shut behind him. The other men, finding the place too quiet, and Mrs Jones unusually taciturn, went into the cool evening air, leaving the landlady to tidy up and sit with the kitten on her knee, staring forlornly at a future that looked almost as bleak as Jasper's.

She got up painfully. If only she could rest her back; but she had no help, and though the men were good, and lugged the barrels for her, they did not help to clean the place and mind the summer visitors, and cook for them, and be up at five, and never in bed till after midnight, and never a break, high day, holiday, Christmas Day, or Sunday, or she'd lose her licence.

101

CHAPTER TWELVE

THE jangling telephone bell, echoing from the amplifier in the yard, called Josh as he was watering the horses. He put the bucket down, cursing. The pipe to the trough was blocked. He'd have to clear it. Too slow to water the beasts by hand.

He stared resentfully at the phone before picking up the receiver, wondering who was assailing his privacy or what message might be waiting. He hated the thing, always made uneasy by it, half fearing bad news.

'Alf Miller here,' said a familiar voice at the other end in reply to his own giving his number. What in tarnation did *he* want?

'Doing you a favour.'

'A favour?' Now Josh was suspicious. What favour could

the knacker do him, unless, as he sometimes did, he was trying to sell him a horse sent to him for slaughter, and a damned bad buy for anyone, as a rule. No one was quite sure whether Alf had a soft heart or an eye for a crooked bargain.

'A favour. Don't sound as I wanted to steal the pigfood.' Alf said, irritable. 'A real favour, Josh, cross my heart.'

'Go on, then,' Josh growled, aware of five horses still unwatered, pigs unfed, and Peg gone into the village shopping and not back till all hours, gossiping in the store.

'Dave Barratt, my boy' – Josh grinned to himself, for Dave was as near sixty as made no odds – 'went South to a Sale, last week. Stopped by a little farm. Rennie's, you know it?'

'Of course I know it,' Josh said irritably. Rennie had bred the Horse of the Year four years ago, Rennie's Magnificence. . . . That had been a horse! Sold to an Australian for breeding, more's the pity, but he'd sired a foal or two before he went.

'Rennie's dead,' Alf said, never getting to the point, but walking all round it, like a hound on a false trail, before he ever told you his business. It annoyed Josh, but he felt a small twinge of pity for old Rennie; he'd been a nice old boy.

'Dave bought Rennie's Beauty. Got by Rennie's Magnificence. Know him?'

Know him? Josh took a deep breath, and then the significance of what Alf was saying dawned on him.

'Dave bought him? A three-year-old? For slaughtering?' His voice jarred Alf's ears, and the knacker held the receiver away from him, grinning to himself. The conversation was going his way.

'Nobody else bid for him. Got him for fifty pounds. Nobody there but Dave and Mick Muggins.'

Josh snorted. Mick Muggins, whose name wasn't Mick Muggins, but Walter Andrews, was a by-word. If he bought a beast it was more than ready for slaughter, it was dead on its feet and had been for months. He got some sorry bargains and never had a penny to spare to bet on horse or hound, or even, some said, to buy anything for himself except the beer that surrounded him with a permanent aura. He had been rechristened Mick Muggins long ago, and the name stuck.

'You can't kill him!'

It was an iniquity. Josh had seen him when he was a foal, with more than a promise of future greatness. Rennie had known about horses, had a masterly touch, bred champion after champion, and been a by-word down South.

'You can have him for fifty-five pounds.'

Josh stared at the calendar on the wall. Peg had given it to him for Christmas, two matched Shires, drawing a plough, gazed from it regally, daring him to condemn their brother to death. He couldn't do it.

'What's the catch?' he asked, knowing the catch, knowing that he had not yet repaid Ted Wellans, and that it had to be done, and there was money owing for feed – there was always money owing for feed – and the blacksmith was due, and a tidy bill for him due too, and Dai needed payment, for the treatment of the Cloud's colic. He could have given the horse a drench himself, but at the last minute his courage failed. It might be worse than he thought, and he kept Dai looking over the beast until they were both sure the Shire had recovered completely.

He looked into the big field, where the new mare grazed with her foal, and old Sally dreamed in the shade under a tree, and Libby ate thistles, deep in donkey bliss.

'I can't pay you, not now,' he said, knowing that Alf would withdraw the offer.

'No need. Keep him till Appledale Fair, and then auction him. There's buyers from all over, and I've heard they're after Shires for breeding and showing. Some foreigners, too. Like the old breeds, and want to keep them going.'

'What's in it for you?' Josh was still suspicious. There

must be a snag to this.

'I don't like killing young, healthy beasts, straight, I don't,' Alf said, not adding that he had been pushed by his father into a trade he despised, and having no other bent, had to keep at it, for the sake of the family, his wife, and three girls still at school. Many men like him, but knacking got him down. He wanted the horse alive, roaming free, not dog-meat on a slab, but he wasn't telling Josh that, not for the life of him. A soft knacker! What would people think?

His voice had been desperate, betraying more than he thought, and Josh took him at his word, but a new thought occurred to him.

'Haven't got room.'

'Put him in Huntsman's paddock,' said Alf, who was local-born, and knew the place well. 'Give the old boy something to do. Looks as if he'd had news of the end of the world, lately, does Huntsman.'

A twinge of regret stirred Josh. He ought to go and see the old man, and find out if anything was being done for him. Besides, they needed him. Nobody else would take over the pack.

'All right,' Josh said, knowing it was far from all right, knowing he was uneasy about the whole deal, knowing that Peg would have plenty to say, knowing that he was too soft by half when it came to the big horses. And suppose Huntsman said no?

His thoughts milled as he went back to his jobs, and then, his conscience still uneasy, he put on the kettle, and when Peg came home on her old rattle-trap bicycle, the basket loaded, he made coffee and put a cup in front of her, on the big white scrubbed kitchen table.

Peg was grateful, and unsuspicious. She stirred the coffee vigorously, although she never took sugar, and sipped contentedly, glad to sit back, watching Libby race the foal round the big field, while his mother watched them amiably.

'Old Rennie's dead,' Josh said.

'That's a shame.' Peg had liked the old man, admiring his big horses, which he had a flair for breeding. She remembered Rennie's Magnificence, a powerfully built and enormous stallion, one of the biggest she'd ever seen.

'Alf's bought Shire from there. Rennie's Beauty.'

'That's the foal we saw three years ago. He's only a baby. Alf can't slaughter him.' Peg stared at Josh, her face horrified. She hated the knacker's trade, and any news of young horses being killed off for no reason always made her furious.

Josh poured more coffee and grinned to himself. For once he'd done it right.

'Gave me an offer of it,' he said casually. 'Told him I'd no room.' Which was true. I did tell him, he thought.

'Room or no room, you can take that horse. How much?' she added hastily, not quite bereft of sense.

'Fifty-five pounds.'

'We'll get more than that for the pigs. Nearly time to sell the baconers. Just tell Alf we'll take the horse.' Peg stood up and went into the yard. Time for egg-collecting. No end to it. She took her basket from the table in the dairy and went into the hen house, where she was greeted by a cackle of rage as old Brownie, who was getting lazy, fled from her nest and went outside to peck irritably at the ground.

'Going to see Huntsman,' Josh called.

'Huntsman?'

'See if he'll have the horse in his paddock. There's good grazing there since Ted took his mare and put her among the cattle. Besides, it'll give the old man something to do. Proper down-in-the-mouth he's looking, lately.'

He strode off into the lane and cut through the path that separated his land from the paddock and orchard that went with the Huntsman's cottage. He looked down at it, made of honeygold stone, and thatched, nestling among a small clump of trees, smothered in climbing roses and clematis and honeysuckle, the garden brilliant with flowers.

As he pushed open the gate, Sung, the Siamese, danced

to greet him with a loud yowl of welcome and waving tail, and Ranger stretched lazily, stood, and thumped a sturdy tail against the green-painted water butt.

The Huntsman was sitting in the shadowy kitchen, where the window was too small to let in much sun. He listened quietly as Josh told him about the Shire.

'Aye. He can come. I'll see to him for you,' the Huntsman said, glad to have something to do, and a more demanding beast to care for than a dog or cat, who were so little trouble he only had to put food down for them when necessary. 'Let's make sure the fence is sound.'

There were weak places, and poisonous ragwort was growing rife. That would have to come out. Astonishing how everything had grown in the few weeks since Ted had removed the mare. The prospect of work was a tonic, and the Huntsman straightened his shoulders and managed a smile.

'It'll be ready,' he promised, and Josh went off to Wellans to see Ted and give him his money back, now they'd decided to keep Burrows' Sensation.

Rob Hinney met him at the gate.

'Best not come in,' he said tersely. His usually pleasant face was grim, and he avoided Josh's startled eyes.

'Why ever not?'

'Because Boss says so. That's why. Nobody's visiting here just now.'

Josh stared at him, bewildered. There was open house at Wellans, always had been. It was not like Ted to turn a neighbour away.

'Look, if Mr Wellans won't let me in, mebbe he could come out,' Josh said reasonably, wondering if Rob were suddenly ill, or even drunk. His manner was most odd, but he didn't smell of beer, and he was a temperate man. Maybe one of his lads was ailing.

'He won't come out, and nobody can come in,' Rob said. 'Look, Mr Johnson, I'm not being awkward. It's just that I've got my orders, and got to keep to 'em.'

'Anyone would think you'd got the plague here,' Josh answered angrily, aware of time wasted, and jobs left undone, and the cheque still burning a hole in his pocket.

To his dismay, Rob's face went grey, the muscles suddenly slack, the eyes desolate.

'Happen we have,' he said, and turned roughtly on his heel, slamming the gate with such violence that he caught Josh's hand in the latch and left him sucking a torn thumb and swearing, his astonished eyes watching as Rob vanished round the corner of the cowshed.

CHAPTER THIRTEEN

RUFF was no longer a dog. He was a wild beast, hunting to kill, without a scrap of affection left for the human race. He had almost forgotten the home that reared him, and had quite forgotten a brief stay with a shepherd who had been kind to him.

Ned, glimpsing him early one evening, stared at the thick matted coat, to which burrs clung, the hooky seeds left after the dog had raced through a clump of burdock. He recognised the breed, knew the fierce eyes, and marked a killer. That would explain the dead lamb at Nick Beston's. More believable than a badger.

A few days after the Show, hunting down towards Tanner's, Ruff found five lambs. Tanner farmed erratically. A few cows, too thin, and yielding little milk, given nothing

109

extra, not even silage, to eke the scrawny grass; chickens that always seemed to be sick, cats and dogs with fleas and worms, pigs that never reared their young; and a few sheep, left to graze where they would, lambing late, to save the chores on cold nights, and not even dipped, if Tanner could get out of it. The Vet kept a wary eye and a sharp tongue for Tanner.

The lambs were easy prey, and hunting them was fun. Ruff picked the smallest, who ran, panic-mad, jumping tussock and clump and rock, circling wildly, bleating desperately, trying to get free. The dog was not in a hurry. He loped, tongue lolling, eyes eager, and ran in leisurely, killing with one bite at the big vein in the throat.

When he had done he left the carcase, and that night, Old Brock, ambling along, weary with age, and without luck in his foraging, took the unexpected gift, and fed well, leaving his own large and noticeable tracks superimposed on the dog's for Tanner to find.

The lamb was disaster. It was a healthy one too. Would have been, Tanner thought sourly, brooding as he often did on the ill luck that dogged him, quite unaware that his own laziness was his enemy. He swore vigorously. He'd have the badger, if no one else did. No one else seemed to care.

That night he took his old gun and crouched against the hedge in the mares' field, but Brock had fed well enough for two days. He had contented himself with a brief sortie on to the fells, where he found a weakly partridge, crouched under a heather clump, ate quickly, drank, and went back to sleep the night through.

Be better by day, Tanner thought morosely. Stop those earths and use gas. Have to pick a time when Josh was out of the way. He'd never know. Time that beast was dead.

Josh himself was watchful, but the badger eluded him although Ned could have told all about its coming and goings. But Ned would never tell. He knew the beast was harmless enough, and was as determined as the schoolmaster that it

110

should survive. Only the night before he had watched Old Brock kill a big rat stalking round Jasper's chicken house.

Twice in the next week Ned saw the dog, running down the wind, ears flattened, tail streaming. Once he glimpsed, sidelong, the wicked eyes, malicious and undog-like, and Ruff came close enough to bare his teeth, lips drawn back, snarling menacingly.

'There's a killer on the moors,' Ned said, later, in the *Swan*, his beer foaming enticingly in front of him. It had been a long hot day, with heavy cloud and distant thunder that rolled threateningly across the brooding hills, so that men and animals were wilful and irritable.

'Dog fox,' Matt Falcon said. 'Lazy devil. Goes for hens. Too much trouble to chase the rabbits and keep them down. Not like last year, when Rufus and Rusty were up on the fells.'

'Never be foxes like those.' The Huntsman's voice was regretful. He sipped his ale slowly, making it last. The days of uncertainty were marking him with a weariness that made him look his age and a few years over. He had seemed ageless before.

'Not a fox, a sheepdog,' Ned said.

'Sheepdog?' Heads turned sharply. Knew what was what, did Ned, whatever his faults. A killer sheepdog was the devil, no mistake, and every man's hand would be against it. Hunted one down with a helicopter, an Alsatian, over Derby way, last spring, but not before sixty sheep had been laid at his door, either dead or worried so much they had to be shot.

'Saw him. Black-and-white, and vicious as they come. Proper nasty snarling brute. Forgotten he's a dog, I reckon. More wolf now. Funny how they can throw back, and forget.'

'Like as not that's what got your lambs, Nick.' The schoolmaster was accepted now, and on first-name terms with the village men. 'People who have worked on badgers have

111

never found a lamb-killer. Eat rabbit and hare, and even earthworms and things like that.'

'There's always rogues.' Tanner was still brooding over his dead lamb. Why couldn't the brute have taken the sick one, the one that had just died of pulpy kidney? No end to the bad luck. 'Same again.'

On another day Mrs Jones would have refused and sent the man packing, but tonight her back was a raw ache, and all her mind was concentrated on keeping going. She served the beer without a word, forgetting that Tanner already had five pints inside him, and no head for the stuff.

'It's the dog that's to blame.' Ned Foley was positive. 'Happen we ought to get after him before he does more damage. The summer visitors are daft about dogs. One woman tried to stroke my Nessie. Glory, there was set-to. Don't let no one touch 'er but me, Ness don't. You'd 'ave thought she'd bitten the woman's arm off, not just growled, from the carry-on. No right to keep a savage beast, she said, No right to stroke a strange dog, and terrify it, Missus, I told her.' He guffawed and drank deep.

'Townsfolk!' Joe Needler had bitter memories of summer visitors who left gates open so that the cattle from the next-door farm ranged far and wide over his nursery garden, trampling plants and vegetables flat. Bad enough to contend with poor soil and rotten summers, and whitefly and blackfly and onion-fly. Whatever man grew there was a fly to plague it, and spray the plants and then the bees died and there was no honey. Between the Government and Nature and the summer visitors, how was a man supposed to live?

'Never mind townsfolk. If there's a killer dog out there, we'd best get after him,' said Nick Beston, reluctant to free the badger from blame, but well aware that Ned was no fool. 'Where's Ted? He's the one to start us off. He's got a rifle.'

Startled faces looked round, realising that Ted Wellans and Rob Hinney, regular visitors for an hour or so each night, savouring rare and well-earned leisure, had not been near all week.

'Busy. Maybe too many cows calving,' suggested the schoolmaster. 'What about the dog?' he added, not liking the idea of hunting it down. 'Couldn't it be caught and given a home?'

'It's hopeless now,' the Huntsman said, and Jasper nodded agreement. They had known many killers. Every year one or two dogs, strayed and hungry, went wild. Sheepdogs and Alsatians were the worst, but even a mongrel could do a power of damage if he'd a mind to.

'Besides,' Jasper added stroking Nell, who had her shining red head, as usual, on his knee, while her brown eyes watched him faithfully, following every movement, 'he might bite one of the little lasses. They go picking wild flowers up on the hills, and they're uncommon trusting when it comes to animals. Stroke anything, some of them, like Jeannie Lee.'

The schoolmaster had a large soft place for Jeannie, who was making immense progress under his gentle care. She could already read the first books in the school, and although she was almost nine, this was, for her, a big achievement. He'd have her able to read and write and take some kind of job yet. He'd be able to cross out the 'mentally deficient, almost moronic' that the last schoolmaster had written against the child's name in his private report book.

He sighed. Pity dogs and people ran amok. It would be nice to live in a world where the only villains were rats and weasels.

Tanner, his brain addled by beer, by brooding, and by thoughts about the badger, blundered to his feet, and went out of the door.

'Half-seas over, is old Tanner,' Ned Foley observed, watching the man's unsteady progress across the room. Painter, having good reason to dislike the surly farmer, who had a way of kicking out or treading deliberately on a paw, growled softly under his breath. Nell turned her head, ears cocked, and gazed thoughtfully at the big hound.

Tanner slammed the door.

'Good riddance,' Josh said sourly. It was time to go, time to give the horses their last feed, and he hadn't put fresh bedding in for the night. Time to go round the place and make sure all was fast and fox-proof and thief-proof, but he wanted a word with the Huntsman first. He changed his seat, shaking his head when Matt Falcon offered to stand him another pint of bitter.

'The Beauty settled in?' he asked. Alf Miller had delivered the horse the day before. Josh and the Huntsman had feasted their eyes, and Josh was glad to see that the young Shire was gentle. He'd been worried lest the newcomer prove a handful, and though Huntsman was strong and could handle any horse, he wasn't a young man any more.

'He's fine. Likes company, and the cat and the dog go visiting.' The Huntsman's wrinkled brown face creased in a sudden smile. 'Put him in the old barn last night, and found the cat sitting there on his back as if she'd grown there. Seemed to like her there. She purred and he grumbled. Funny noise it was too.'

'Sort of groan,' Josh said, remembering other horses that had made the same sound. He'd never known whether it was pain or pleasure.

'Seen anyone from Wellans?' he asked, remembering his odd encounter with Rob Hinney, a day or so before.

The rank blue smoke wreathed towards the rafters. Mrs Jones eased herself wearily from the bench and began to gather glasses, her face marked with pain. Jo Needler whistled his hound and went out into the evening air. A waft of fragrance from the honeysuckle outside in the hedge drifted through the door and vied with the tobacco scent. The Huntsman began to speak, and then thinking again, changed his mind and said something else.

'Happen I'd better not say what I were going to say,' he

answered at last, his eyes, puzzled, watching the landlady as she dragged herself round the room. 'There's trouble, I think. Bad trouble. But until we're sure, words and rumours could make it worse.'

Josh looked at him, and frowned, his thoughts on polio and divorce, and other tragedies. He shrugged, whistled Jess who was busy making friends with Ranger, and went out into the lane.

The sun was almost gone, and lay in a flare of last light on the streaky clouds, black streamers lying in a pool of flame. He looked at the hills, humped and featureless against the sky, darkness drifting over their flanks. A swallow, late home, dipped across his head, and flew into the eaves of the *Swan*, where a twitter from the youngsters greeted its coming.

A hedgehog ambled out of the ditch, stared in astonishment at the giant that confronted it, head bent to examine it, and then made off at speed, its legs projecting improbably from a body as graceless as a child's drawing.

Josh gave a deep sigh, welcoming peace, and the cool breeze that succeeded the day. Soon his Shires would be winning prizes again. He began to whistle 'Billy Boy,' and strode off homewards, the bitch following, now at this heels, now running eagerly ahead sniffing at the ditch.

She smelled danger before he did. Her nose quivered as she sniffed the air. She whimpered, came running back to Josh and pushed anxiously at his hand, trying to alert him. His thoughts were busy, but as they turned the corner of the bend in the lane, smoke drifted across his nostrils and the smell of burning caught at his throat. Jess whimpered again.

Terror followed the realisation of fire. Josh began to run. Jess ahead of him, and then, as fear caught up with her, dropping behind. His heavy footsteps thundered on the ground.

CHAPTER FOURTEEN

SMOKE poured across the farmyard, black and pungent.
Josh ran through it, choking, his heart thumping. Did it
come from barn or stack or stable, or from the house itself?
And where was Peg? And what about the horses? Cursing
himself for tarrying, he yelled for his wife.

'I'm in the field,' Peg called, and he was almost sick with
relief.

He pushed open the gate, eyes smarting. There was an
odd acrid tang in the air, and he thrust his way through
smoke that poured towards him, quite unable to make
out its source.

'Thank God you're here,' Peg's voice greeted him.

He pulled out a handkerchief and wiped his smarting
eyes. He was beyond the smoke, and was astounded to see

Peg holding the shotgun, of which, he knew, she was terri-fied, and Tanner, grey-faced and shaking, facing her.

'Tell 'er I didn't mean no 'arm,' he shouted desperately at Josh, but without much hope.

'Harm?' Peg almost exploded. 'He tried to kill the badger. Filled the sett entrance with tarred sacks and straw and soaked the lot in petrol and then set light to it, and Libby and Sally still in the field.'

'What about the Shires?' It was all Josh could think of.

'They're all safe in the stables,' Peg said, her voice im-patient. 'Knew what you were like, once you got down to the *Swan*. But Libby's run off, fair terrified, and I don't know what happened to Sal. Jumped the gate like a two-year-old and she's away, Lord only knows where.'

'You're a . . .' Words choked Josh. He stared at the last dull shreds of flame, coming from the corner of the field. The smell of tarred sack and petrol and burning straw was indescribable. His throat was raw, and his eyes stung. He took Tanner by the collar, and the man pulled away and shouted to be let alone.

'You miserable drunken little oaf.' Josh's voice was a bull bellow. 'Peg, put that damned gun away and get indoors.'

Peg went, not inside, but anxiously, to the stables, where the horses were restless, and the Cloud stood, hating the drifting smoke. He tossed his head, mane flying, when he saw her. She hesitated, wondering how much smoke would drift through if she locked the top half of the stable door. She decided to leave it open. The smoke would clear. There was no sign of Libby or Sal.

'Your donkey kicked me. Near broke me arm.' Tanner's voice was a sorry whine. He was stone cold sober, with the awful realisation that comes to the drunkard when he comes to his senses too soon after his binge.

'Pity she didn't break your neck, and save me the trouble,' Josh said. He had a firm grip on Tanner's collar, and took another on the man's wrist, a grip that almost paralysed. Tanner cringed.

'I didn't mean no 'arm. Wanted to get the badger. Been after me lambs. Killed the best one. You wanted it dead too,' he added with the brilliant improvisation of the terrified. 'Doing you a good turn.'

'You might 'ave panicked all the horses, and set fire to the stack, let alone the stables and house,' Josh said, his voice deceptively gentle. 'You seen where that stack is?'

Tanner shook his head.

Josh walked him down the field, and out through the gate, and round the corner and into the next field. Standing on the headland they surveyed the remnants of last year's rick, which stood against the hedge, trails of straw lying around, some pulled there by the tame stag that visited many of the farms, and some pulled by Libby, who had a genius for getting into any place that attracted her.

'Suppose that 'ad gone up? And the wind the way it is, and my stables just over there? You flaming maniac,' Josh roared suddenly, and flung the man away from him so that he fell in the straw, staring pitifully, wondering what was going to happen next.

'Want to charge him?'

Ben Timmins, the policeman, who had been cycling past and smelled smoke and heard the tale from Peg, walked ponderously across the field. He was a big man, his uniform straining across his burly body, his flourishing moustache helping him to show a fierce face to little naughty boys, and hiding the mild and smiling mouth beneath it. He had seen Josh fling the farmer on to the ground, but decided to be temporarily blind, feeling angry himself at such a tomfool trick, drunk or not drunk.

'I want to break his ruddy neck,' Josh said.

'Brought your donkey back,' Ben Timmins said, feeling this statement was better ignored. He was a farmer's son himself, and had a few pigs and chickens and a cow, though his wife did most of the chores, these days.

He could help in winter, but there always seemed to be the odd bit of trouble with summer visitors. And how their kids got lost! He couldn't think how they managed it. When it wasn't kids, it was dogs, and a man camping down Windy Hollow had managed to lose a cat, if you please. Ben was always baffled by the goings-on of holiday-makers.

'Seen old Sal?'

Ben shook his head.

'Come on, Tanner. Drunk and disorderly, and setting fire to property to the public danger. See what the magistrate has to say to that.' It wasn't quite the right phrasing, but it sounded near enough. Ben had never had such a case before.

'Oh, leave it!' Josh was suddenly sick of the whole business, and not anxious to be on even worse terms with his neighbour. They'd both got to live in the place. 'Get him out of here, and drop it. Though if he sets foot on my land again, I'll let Peg use that gun. She never could shoot straight, and he'll live to be sorry.'

Ben Timmins winked at Josh, and took Tanner off, trying to talk sense into the man, as he walked beside him, wheeling his heavy bicycle. The smallholder, abashed and ashamed, and knowing that he would never have acted so if he had been sober, shuffled along wearily, avoiding Peg's eyes as he passed the farmhouse door.

Josh went into the stables. He checked over the stallions, and then the mares. Silver, whose foal was soon to be born, was drooping, and next to her the foal, Bruton Hope, was breathing uneasily. The place reeked of burning tar.

'Never rains but it pours,' Josh said furiously. 'Come on, Peg. Silver and Hope need air. This place is full of smoke.'

'There's Jess,' Peg said, leading the foal outside, and taking him across the yard, where he could stand in the cool night breeze and breathe as if breathing was something new to him, a pleasure long denied. The bitch crept out from behind the Land-Rover, wagging an anxious tail.

'Sent for Dai,' she added. 'Thought he'd best look at them,

and Libby's in a state. Lamed herself. Put her hoof in a rabbit hole, I shouldn't wonder. Ben found her on the bridle path, staring at a hedgehog as if she thought it'd eat her.'

Josh looked at the big mare anxiously. She was less distressed, and she stood quietly, long shuddering breaths subsiding into a more reasonable rhythm.

'Who'd 'a' thought Tanner'd do a damn fool thing like that?' Josh asked, still unable to credit it.

'Hope the badger wasn't there.' Peg rubbed her face against the foal's warm velvety neck, as it lifted its head to look at her. 'It's a cruel way to die.'

'He thought smoke'd go into the earth and drive badger out so that he could shoot it,' Ben Timmins said, coming back, having sent Tanner on his way with a threat of jail next time. 'Won't do that in a hurry again. Trouble was, smoke came out instead of in.'

'I dunno.' Josh pushed his hand through his red hair. It stood up spikily from his skull, giving him the appearance of a crested bird. 'Reckon Tanner's daft, sometimes.'

'Came to say Sal's in a pond on Jo Needler's land. The one beyond his big greenhouse. Put her foot through a cucumber frame and reckon it's cut bad, poor beast, judging by the blood trail. The men from the motorway are getting her out. Dai's stopped off there.' Ben nodded ponderously and patted Silver before walking away.

'Best get down there, I suppose,' Josh said.

'Best not leave this pair till Dai's seen them.' Now the excitement was over, her legs were shaking, and Peg felt sick. Suppose she had accidentally shot Tanner?

'Better unload the gun, anyway.' Josh was meticulous about his weapons, knowing of too many accidents through carelessness with loaded guns.

'Unload it?' Peg stared at him as if he were out of his mind.

'You did load it?'

Peg shook her head. Josh began to laugh.

'You never thought I'd leave a gun loaded?' he asked.

'I never thought . . . ' Peg's voice trailed away. She was dead tired, and if they didn't get to bed it would be milking time again. She saw nothing to laugh at.

Dai's Land-Rover stopped outside, and the Vet climbed out, his face glum. He walked over, and without a word, began to look at the mare and the foal.

'No harm done to them, not that I can see at the moment, anyway,' he said, his examination completed. He sniffed. There was still a trace of smoke about. 'You charging Tanner?'

Josh shook his head.

'What about old Sal?' It was all Peg could think about now.

'You ought to charge Tanner.' Dai picked up the foal's hoof and examined it. 'He'll soon be ready for shoeing. Time goes fast.' He walked over to Libby, who shivered her ears and greeted him with a cold nose, rubbed into his neck. She adored the little Welshman, and stood quietly while he examined her leg, and dismissed her with a lump of sugar and a pat.

Peg looked at Josh in dismay.

'Something's wrong!'

She did not need telling. Dai walked into the house. Josh put the mare and the foal into an empty stable, away from the smoke. He gave them both hay to comfort them, and gentled and fed Libby and went back to find Dai stretched out in a chair. Cappy sat on one knee, and Marmie on the other, while Tinker, on the hearthrug, washed his hind leg ardently, leaning against Jess to keep his balance.

Peg poured a stiff whisky for each man, but Dai refused his, having at least five other calls to make, so that Peg drank it for him.

'Out with it,' she said, dreading what she was to hear, yet wanting to get it over.

'They meant well,' Dai started unhappily. 'But they'd

122

never pulled a horse out of anywhere before. Just labourers. The rope slipped. Broke her neck.'

Peg went out into the kitchen, taking her glass with her. She stared miserably at the whitewashed wall. Old Sal, whom they'd had for twenty-eight years, ever since she was foaled, part of life, and dear as any human. Dearer than many. Peg thought, with a sour memory of Tanner cowering in front of her.

Silly to mind, but she did mind. She stood in the dark, the white walls gleaming faintly, mourning for the old mare, whose head would never push against her arm again, whose galloping hooves would never speed to greet her when she came to the field. Old Sal, the thief horse, who would never again come to the open kitchen window and steal new bread.

Dai came out into the darkness.

'I'd have had to put her down in any case, Peg,' he said. 'She'd cut herself so badly, I think she'd almost bled to death.'

Peg didn't answer, nor did she hear him leave. Poor old Sal, to die among strangers, terrified, because a drunken fool had tried to kill a harmless beast that lived on their land.

'Come to bed, lass,' Josh said, his voice unusually gentle.

Sal had been Peg's own horse. The lads had learned to ride on her. He could see them now, absorbed, riding round the field. He missed them. Could do with them on the farm, but you couldn't tie them down, not all their lives. Funny, they'd had the mare before any of the boys were born. Almost all their married lives. She'd remained when the lads had left home. Part of the family.

Peg lay in the darkness, remembering how Sally had come to her, only that evening, bright and full of mischief, and taken the mash that was meant for Silver. The moon had vanished, and day dawned, grey and miserable, the wind whipping clouds across a tattered sky, before sleep came to her.

Outside, the badger came home and went into the earth that he had left at dawn the day before. He had slept high on the moors, visiting a deserted sett, and been far away when Tanner came. He sniffed, smelled strangeness, and backed away, growling deep in his throat.

Peg, getting up, unrefreshed and miserable, knowing that Sal would not be waiting to greet her with joy, saw him amble towards the fells, a little broad bear, lonely and seeming desolate as he went to find new sanctuary.

'All for nothing,' she thought. And wondered if the badger really was ill luck. Nothing went right these days, goodness knew why.

CHAPTER FIFTEEN

'SHE'LL be all right now.' Dai stood beside Bruton Silver, his hands gentle on her warm neck. She acknowledged him with a movement of her ears, and her long-lashed dark eyes watched him as he packed his bag. Her head drooped wearily.

Dai had been with her since three that morning, when Josh, anxious for no reason that he could give, had gone down to look at her, and found her restless and uneasy, about to foal, and at that six weeks too soon.

Peg, coming into announce that coffee was ready when they were, saw the dead foal lying in the yard, waiting for Alf Miller, and her mouth tightened. Damn Tanner. Damn damn, damn Tanner.

'What happened night before last, Peg?'

Dai watched her, his eyes sombre, his mind on another job already, a job that he loathed.

'The smoke came into the stables. All the horses were nervous, and Silver reared and plunged for a minute or two before I got to her and shifted her to another loose box, out of the reek.'

Dai nodded.

'Knocked herself, and terrified. She's hurt her leg, too. Gone lame. Didn't show up before. Must have knocked against something sharp. Possibly kicked herself with her own shoe. Not all that bad, but need to watch it. Sorry, Josh.'

'Not your fault,' Josh was sponging the mare, and Peg brought her warm gruel, but she turned her head away. Dai observed her, frowning. She was fretting for the foal. He had seen her looking down at the straw, puzzled, as if she thought it was buried there. Twice she pawed uneasily, pulling away the straw from the floor beneath her, as if trying to expose the tiny creature, sure it must be hidden. This was her third foal, and she was an excellent mother. A beautiful grey. The foal had been grey, too. The Vet sighed.

He went in for coffee, but Peg could get no word out of him, and finally left him to finish cleaning up after milking, already behind with her day. She had left the cows in the confined yard behind the milking parlour when Josh called her. She let them into the field, and sighed as she looked at the mess. She fetched the hose.

Dai watched her with a dark face, took his disreputable hat, nodded, and went off, unnoticed, to his Land-Rover, almost wrenching off the gear lever in savage anger as he turned and sped along the lane towards Wellans.

He was dead tired and defeated. The foal was a nasty blow for Josh. He seemed to be having a run of bad luck lately. All due to the badger? Dai knew the gossip and snorted. As if a beast could bring ill-luck!

He braked to a standstill on the high curve of the winding road that bisected the fells. There was not a house in sight, though if he had binoculars he would be able to see Wellans' twisted chimneys rising out of massed trees that sheltered

126

the old stone Elizabethan house from the bleak icy winds that swept down the fell in winter.

There was solace on the fells. And a curlew calling, its soft liquid trill plaintive. Two buzzards circled high, brown wings beating in unison. One of them plunged. A moment later the second joined it, and Dai let in his clutch and sighed. Even here, peace was an illusion. He wondered what small beast had suffered sudden death.

The car outside Wellans was familiar, and so was the man who sat in it, shoulders hunched and face brooding. Sergeant Henty, from Horton.

'Waited for you,' he said, disentangling himself from the vehicle, which enclosed his huge bulk with the neat fit of a glove. He dwarfed the car as he stood beside it.

Dai merely nodded, thanking him for nothing.

'Let's get it over, for God's sake,' he went on, in a small explosion of violence. 'Rob says he's practically certain now. Only a hunch before.'

The house was deserted. There was no fire in the kitchen, no sign of Mrs Wellans or the children, no cattle in the empty milking parlour. Their plaintive note could be heard from a field behind the house, where a rope barred access to the gate.

Ted, unshaven, unkempt, his face grey and exhausted, met them.

'All right,' he said, 'Get it over. No need to tell me. Guessed a couple of days ago. But not enough to go on.'

Dai went into the stall, where Sheba lay, lack-lustre, eyes glazing, worse since yesterday, strings of saliva hanging from her mouth. Her coat was harsh with illness. In only a day or so, she had turned the corner, heading straight downhill to death.

'It is, isn't it?' Ted asked, his eyes on the beast, on her distressed panting, on his former triumph exposing her to danger for the sake of a piece of paper and a silver cup.

'That damned Show,' he said bitterly.

'You couldn't know. I rang Derry's after your phone call to me. Foot-and-mouth was confirmed there two days ago, and he'd forgotten that Sheba was next to his cow at the Show. He didn't think his winner was affected, but she must have been. Have to find out how it started over there.'

'His cow must have been infected. How else could Sheba have got it?' Ted had no heart in his voice.

'Man who handled Derry's cows could 'ave carried the virus. Or feedstuffs. That's often how it gets from farm to farm. Ministry men will be here soon, and two slaughterers. I got in touch at once.' Dai wanted to be miles away. 'Your sheep are well away, up on the fells, and Tom doesn't come down here, does he?'

Ted shook his head. 'Deer carry it. Does that stag come here?'

Ted's heart seemed to knot inside him and then untie again with a twinge that made him sick. The children's stag, which came almost daily to be hand-fed, and then went the round of the other farms, taking hay from this one, a browse at the stack from that one, visiting Josh's cattle, and Jasper's five cows, with splendid impartiality.

'Aye,' he said slowly, with feeling akin to treachery. The kids were sore enough about the cattle. Surely the stag couldn't be infected already? But sometimes it only took a few days.

Dai set his mouth. He knew the stag. His own children ran to greet it and bring it apples, which it took from their hands, gentle, and trusting, except in the rutting season, when it vanished, only to return, thinner and worn, a few weeks later, and resume its old life. Jeannie Lee petted it, holding hay to it, her eyes bright with wonder because a wild animal from the forests came visiting her.

'It will have to go,' Dai said, his voice colourless, his own feelings clamped beneath a professional mask.

Rob Hinney came into the yard, his heavy boots noisy on the cobbles. His normally red face was redder than usual, his voice thick, and the sergeant, looking at him startled, realised that, early as it was, he had been drinking. Must have brought the beer with him. Not like Rob.

The cowman stared at them, tense with anger.

'Kill every beast, that's the Government, isn't it, never mind whether they're sick or well. Ought to let us have injections against it, like they do on the Continent.'

'Can't argue, Rob. It's got to be wiped out, and this is the only way we know,' Dai said.

'The only way you want to know.' Rob came forward, fists clenched. 'Don't care, do you? Only cows, and not your cows, I've looked after those cows since they were born. Nursed 'em, fed 'em, milked 'em. I know their pedigrees, every one of them, right back, twenty years back. I know every cow, every last one. And now you're going to kill them all. Just in case.'

'Come on, Rob. Best come home,' the Sergeant said, and to his immense surprise found himself on the ground, with Rob driving a fist towards him, ready to lash out again.

'Oh, hell,' Ted said helplessly, and grabbed at the cowman, who stood, suddenly deflated, his hands hanging by his sides, his face sullen. Dai and Ted looked away, avoiding each other's eyes.

'Come on, Rob home to bed.' The Sergeant had scrambled up, and spoke as if to a small child, and the cowman followed him meekly, the fight gone from him, the maudlin self-pity of drunkenness left.

'Can't think what's got into Rob,' Ted said, knowing perfectly well. The man had not been sober for two days.

He walked away, away from the house and the sight of the cows, taking his gun up on to the fells, where he blazed off at rabbits. He did not wait for the slaughterers with their humane killers, nor return until it was time for lunch, to find the gates chained, with notices which read 'Keep Out,' the beasts dead, and smoke blackening the sky.

Bess Logan was grim when she spoke to Jasper.

'Foot-and-mouth at Wellans,' she said.

Jasper looked at her, appalled, unable to answer, and she rubbed a hand irritably over her face and walked away, while he went to look at Lou and Twitchett, at Rosie and Heather, and Bluebell, and wonder anxiously if they were well, or already sickening. He'd had no contact with Ted, not since the Show, a brief nine days ago, and he guessed that had brought it. There'd been a cattle standstill order the other side of Coniston, three days after the Show, and Derry's was over that way. Jim Derry's shorthorn, Sarabelle, he remembered, had come second to Sheba and in the next pen. Derry's cowman, Hodge, had fed both cows during the long day.

Peg, going down to the village, found the women standing, grave-faced, in the store. This could affect all of them, for scarcely a household lacked one or two cows, and many had small herds. Even Mrs Jones kept two Jerseys in her big orchard, for milk, and for cream. And pigs were vulnerable. And sheep.

She came back with her purchases. Josh was standing beside Bruton Silver, trying to get the grey mare to feed, but she was listless. She seemed well enough, but she was fretting her heart out. He tried hand-feeding her gruel in a cupped hand, but she turned her head away and would have none of him, suffering his stroking hand in silence, but not responding.

'They've foot-and-mouth at Wellans,' Peg said, without preamble.

Josh stared at her, his own face whitening, thinking of his Friesians. Fifty of them, all pedigree. Dear God, had he brought the virus on his shoes with him that day he went down to pay Ted?

'That accounts for it.' He was thinking of Rob's refusal to let him in and his grey face when Josh mentioned the plague

Must have been suspicious, even then. Took time to diagnose. Just off their feed at first, like any other illness.

'Accounts for what?'

Peg was never to learn, for a voice behind her made her jump.

'Dai asked me to look in. He's acting for the Ministry, so he's got to stand by at Wellan's. But he's worried about your mare. Says she's fretting. I'm John Paterson. From over beyond Horton.'

'She's fretting all right, Mister.' Josh turned to see a tall thin man, heavy horn-rimmed spectacles hiding his eyes. His blond hair was cut square at the neck, and short, almost fringed, in front. He looked painfully young, Josh thought.

He moved forward with assurance, examining Silver thoroughly.

'She's a winner.' His voice was enthusiastic. He preferred horses to any other animals, wished he had lived in the old days when every man of substance kept his own. He still had his own childhood pony, unable to bear to part with him to a stranger, or shoot him while he was strong and healthy. Merry was too fat, and a little pernickety and spiteful with age, but Paterson liked him in the paddock; liked caring for him.

'She's not ailing?'

John Peterson shook his head.

'Got a favour to ask,' he said diffidently. 'The Colonel's Binnie foaled three days ago. She died yesterday. They're hand-feeding the foal. Worth a small fortune. Half-Arab was Binnie, and the sire's all Arab. He hopes to race the youngster. Good blood in him. Wondered if you'd foster the foal ... if Silver will take it ... Help you, and he'll be grateful – more than grateful. Worth a try?'

'Well worth a try. She's still in milk.'

'I'll get them to send it over. I'd like to see your other Shires.'

131

The stallions were in the paddocks. Bruton Cloud came at his master's call, eager for fussing, his head pushing amiably at Josh's shoulder, and then dipping to the hand that produced a carrot for him, leaving the familiar at once for the stranger, so that John Paterson laughed.

'Greedy thing.'

'Greedy as they come,' Josh said, looking at his horse, never tiring of the deep dapple-grey colouring, the white, now muddy, on the magnificent legs. The Cloud had snatched another carrot. He'd eat anything, even bread, and some picnicker had once fed him with beef sandwiches, which he took avidly, much to Josh's astonishment.

Like poor old Sal. She'd eat anything left in reach. It was odd not to see her in the field, and Libby was fretting;

round and round the field, on that first day alone, the little donkey had gone, all morning, as if hunting for Sal, who had been her constant companion for ten years.

Bruton Ebony and Bruton Sable, both with their three white socks discoloured by mud, were less willing to be handled by a stranger, but both came to Josh, the Ebony calling a greeting from the other side of the paddock, and coming with a thunder of hooves on the hard ground, wanting nothing but a pat on his neck and a friendly word. He refused his carrot until Josh took it and offered it himself.

The Sable came more slowly, showing his paces, wary, not liking strangers at all. His black coat gleamed in the sunlight that escaped from a break in heavy cloud, and brought a ray of promise into a bleak landscape.

His mane lifted, and he broke into a trot, swept his head down and towards Josh, suddenly anxious for a caress, for the touch of a human hand. The Sable loved Josh handling him, revelled in the smooth sweep of the brush on his coat, stood patiently enduring ministrations to his mane and tail, and never failed to give thanks in his own way, rubbing silken lips against Josh's bearded face.

Smoke beyond Wellans grew in a pall. It brooded over the sky, darkened the day, drove pleasure away. John Paterson, seeing it, set his lips. This one ill no Vet could cure, as yet.

'Best be on my way.'

He drank Peg's coffee hastily, and drove off down the lane, where, on the next straight stretch, Mary Wellans overtook him in her little grey Morris driving like a fiend, foot down, hand on the horn.

'Told you to keep away,' her husband said angrily, as she came in through the gate. He had sent her to her mother, the other side of Coniston, with the children.

'I knew you wouldn't feed, and the other men need food,' Mary answered. She unloaded the car and went indoors, taking pies and buns with her. She relit the fire, and took a duster to the rooms, but the sounds outside were more than she could bear. When the men came in, one at a time, to gulp scalding coffee, their own faces dark and set, and eat hurriedly, tears she could no longer hide rolled down her cheeks and starred the plates as she handed them their meal.

CHAPTER SIXTEEN

THE smoke above Wellans died away, but fear remained. The gates were closed, the chickens shut up, even the dogs and cats had to be isolated, lest they took the virus from infected ground on their paws and contaminated others.

The sheep, luckily sent to summer on high ground, and far enough away, remained, and Tom Ladyburn was thankful. Even so, he checked them constantly, watching their feet for blistering, careful to find out the cause of any lameness.

Rob Hinney, unable to go anywhere because of contact with the infected cattle, brooded at home, digging violently over Mag's garden, shouting at the children when they made a noise, so unlike himself that the younger ones cowered away from him, and his elder son spent less and less time at home, anxious to avoid his father. After his one lapse,

Rob swore off the drink. He was bitterly ashamed of his outburst.

Ted, with the help of men sent by the Ministry, disinfected everything; byres and yard and stables, burning the stacks from which the cattle had fed, destroying the clothes that he and Rob had worn. When all was done he took his family abroad for the first holiday they had had together for years, unable to face the empty fields and the silence. Dai took the dogs and cats and isolated them at his home, an old house with plenty of outbuildings. Rob fed the chickens, and brooded.

He had never known disease strike so hard before. The herd had been his life and pride, each one known by name, by nature, and by her pedigree. Sweet-tempered Dulcibel, little spiteful Jezebel, well-named proud Sheba, the best of them all, and several times a winner at Dairy Shows. They had known him and come to him happily for feeding and for milking, shown him their calves with pride, all of them born on the farm and grown to maturity there, each one's ancestry on the tip of his tongue. Sheba's six daughters had gone, and Majesty, the bull, and the pig sties were as empty as the byres.

The village brooded too. Worry had only just begun for them. The virus could be carried by bird and by beast, by hedge-hog, stag, or visiting dog. It became even more important to hunt down the killer dog, and the badger was suspect too.

Had he walked through the field where Sheba lay, before her illness became apparent, and then trudged across Josh's pasture? And Jasper's? And Tanner's? Each man watched his cows constantly, examining feet and mouth for tell-tale blisters, wondering if this one was off her food, or that one had the first glaze of sickness in her eyes. It would be a fortnight before they knew for sure. The incubation period varied so.

Summer visitors trespassing in the fields found short shrift.

136

Their shoes could carry the plague, and they were warned off angrily by all the farmers around. Full compensation did not make up for farms without stock for weeks, or the loss of milk, or of favoured animals. New milking stock would need to be bought, pedigrees that had been cherished for a generation or more were abruptly ended. No more daughters of Majesty, the Wellans' bull, would walk in the meadows; none of Sheba's calves had survived to carry on the strain of good milk yields and fine calves.

Long faces were the order of the day, and the atmosphere at the *Swan* was sullen, each man worrying lest he should have stayed away, lest his neighbour's cattle were already sickening, and he might carry the germ home. No man thought that disaster would strike directly at him.

Until at last only the Huntsman sat by himself in the chimney corner with Ranger beside him, and one of Bess Logan's tomcat's many kittens on his knee.

Mrs Jones, relaxing for the first time for weeks, eased herself into the big chair, having made a cup of tea.

'Been thinking,' she said.

It was not an easy thing to say. She was an independent woman and not given to asking help. And the Huntsman might resent her words.

'There's the annex. Not used. make a cosy home if you'd a mind. And I need help here. Too much for me, with me back bad. Doctor says I'll have to lie up and take things easy.'

The Huntsman stared at her, startled.

'You want me to move into the annex?'

'Only if you've a mind to. Thought.... Mebbe.... Don't want to interfere. It'd not be like your own home, nothing would, but you could keep your animals, and have a bit of peace. Better than the Home.'

The Huntsman could find nothing to say.

'You could still lead the hounds,' Mrs Jones added, afraid he was offended, afraid he would turn her offer down, afraid

137

that she would lose her last chance of keeping on as landlady of the *Swan*. It was not easy to get temporary replacements. The brewery might refuse to have her back, afraid that her health would not allow her to keep going.

The Huntsman could still say nothing. Life had been desolate, with nowhere to go but the Home in the town, away from the fells and the hounds and the men he'd lived with, his whole life through.

'Forget it if you want to.' Mrs Jones turned her head to the fire, hiding the disappointment in her eyes.

Blue smoke hit the Huntsman's face. He patted Ranger, and then shifted his hand to the tiny bony body of the kitten, featherlight, warm upon his knee, its minute purr, throbbing frenziedly as it felt caressing human hands.

'Dunno what to say,' the Huntsman answered at last. 'You sure it's all right?'

'Spoke to Mr Betwick himself. He thought it a good idea, if you'd a mind to come.'

Bill Betwick was local too. Born in the house built by his grandfather, an extraordinary mock Tudor mansion with pillars and porticos, with an immense ballroom with a musicians' gallery and fretworked pillars painted in blue and gold. A family monstrosity, now run as a Youth Hostel. But Bill loved the villages and knew the folk. A good man, and an understanding one. He had been worried about Mrs Jones, not wanting to replace her, yet knowing the work was getting beyond her. Seemed a good idea all round.

'He said he'd get it done over,' Mrs Jones went on, referring to the annex, which she classed in her own mind as a right tip, used as a store-room and dumping ground, and not decorated or properly cleaned up in all the time she'd been at the *Swan*. 'Three rooms, and there's gas laid on in the little room where the sink is. You can have that for your kitchen. Be quite separate like. And Mr Betwick says if you'll help out he'll forget about the rent. It's been standing idle all these years. Just use it for stores, and they can go in the cellar.'

The pipe went out, and the Huntsman managed a smile that proved his feeling better than words. It was not much substitute for his own cottage, with the view over the fells, the snug thatched roof, and the garden he had cherished for years, and he did not know that he really wanted to help at the *Swan*.

But it was better than leaving the village, better than one room in a Home full of old men, unimaginably better than leaving Ranger and the Siamese. It would be a place of his own, where he was needed and not merely tolerated, put away to endure life until he died. As he stood to go, his smile, this time, was heartfelt.

He left Mrs Jones feeling happier than she had done for weeks. He had the Shire to feed. He promised to come in next day and made a start on cleaning the annex, and also to give a hand at lunchtime, and clear up for her so that she could rest in the afternoon.

His step was light and his head held high when he met Josh, who was coming to look at the Beauty.

'Going to move into Mrs Jones' annex and help out at the *Swan*,' the Huntsman said, satisfaction suddenly seeping into his voice as he realised that he would not have to spend the rest of his life cooped up in one room in a strange town.

Josh stared at him, and then grinned, the first grin for days. He could think of nothing apt to say, but the Huntsman knew his thoughts. They stood side by side, smoking companionably, watching the Shire graze. Seeing them, the big horse came across for conversation.

'Good job, you took him on,' Josh said, 'Pay you rent for your field, mind. If I'd had him home I'd never've had the heart to sell him.'

'You're still selling him?' The rent would come in handy. Josh meant it well. The Huntsman would have a little more spare cash now, if he was getting the annex free. They'd not regret it, he'd see to that. He was still spry for all his years.

'Aye. Hope to get a good price for him. Take him to Appledale to the Beast Sale. Jack Hinney says there's some Americans coming over, wanting a Shire stallion. Was going to sell one of mine, but can't bear to. Rather shoot them than let them go to strangers who might ill-treat them.'

The Huntsman grinned in his turn. Josh was a by-word in Bruton when it came to his Shires.

'Cattle all well?' The Huntsman shared the fears of the villagers.

Josh nodded, his thick red fingers crossed.

'Three more days left to go,' he said heavily. 'And then Dai shot the stag yesterday, on my land. Deer can get foot-and-mouth, and carry it. Last year, in North Wales they had to kill cattle on ten farms, and then go out and shoot every one of a herd of deer that used to come and steal the grazing. Only hope the old stag's not been feeding at Wellans'. Now Dai says we'd better count another fortnight before we're sure.' He sighed. 'Felt sorry for that poor stag. Peg used to feed and pet him. He trusted us.'

The Huntsman also knew the stag. It had been round the place for three years or more, a solitary animal, an outcast, perhaps or strayed from a park. He had never seen it with other deer, but it always vanished in the rutting season.

They knew it in the spring, when, its head oddly bare, it came looking for hay to eke out the poor feeding; they knew it in late summer, when the dead velvet hung in ragged streamers, and it thrashed against the woody heather stems, and rubbed against the trees; and in winter, when it came demanding, delicate-footed and friendly, into the yards, knocking with its curved antlers on doors and windows, imperious, knowing that food would be forthcoming. And now it, too, was dead.

'Time the luck changed,' the Huntsman said, thinking of his good fortune, and wishing that the whole village could participate. Wishing that Jasper, too, might find a solution to his own problem, for the old man was becoming even crankier, and had no good word for anyone, not even Huntsman, his oldest friend.

CHAPTER SEVENTEEN

OLD BROCK left the sett on Jasper's land, unable to stand the stench that drifted through it. It was alien and unpleasant, the air dead and poisonous, and he climbed to a new home on the fells, left by badgers many years before, and tenanted at intervals by foxes.

He spent the night enlarging the entrance, and clearing the earth, ready for habitation. Ned Foley, fancying a stolen and illegal partridge for his dinner next day, saw him come backwards out of the ground, the old bedding packed against his chest, held by his front paws. He left it in an untidy heap and foraged busily, making the most of the brief grey light before dawn.

The partridge could wait. Ned watched with amusement, seeing the badger come backwards, his load of bracken fronds held with care. He shuffled along anxiously, vanishing, striped face last, into his tunnel entrance. It took him a long time to make his home to his satisfaction, and it was well after daylight when Ned left, and found his partridge still stupid with sleep at the edge of a covey sheltering in a fallow field. He shot it cleanly, the sound echoing in the silence that followed the noisy chorus at dawn.

He went home with his trophy under his coat, the gun carefully hidden high on the fells, lest anyone question his licence, and also realised that he had been infringing the game laws. Ned did not believe in obeying the Government, or the book, which was only written by men like him.

He knew that the badger should have been shot, but thought that the old beast would remain on the fells, where it could not infect cattle. If indeed it was a carrier, a fact which he doubted, having his own opinions about germs.

The next night Old Brock, feeling hungry, left his new home, and quested high among the tussocky heather. He found little, and went lower, coming upon a recently killed, well-grown lamb, which Ruff had taken the morning before. The dog, vicious with frequent hunger, a sore shoulder which had not healed properly, because there was still shot festering inside, and an ever-growing pain in his head, was becoming fiercer. Now, not bothering to hunt fresh quarry, he returned to his previous kill.

He saw the badger, and snarled.

Brock turned swiftly, head lowered, and growled viciously. He was hungry too, and he had only just begun to feed, and he was first at the kill and unaware that the dog had best title.

Ruff circled, aware that this beast would not prove such easy game as helpless lambs and small rabbits. Stiff-legged, growling, he backed away, and then walked slowly forwards, hoping that the menace in voice and appearance would scare the badger into running.

Brock had no intention of giving up his supper. His small

head weaved from side to side. The dog raced in, bit, and backed away, but not before a heavy paw had slashed down on his shoulder, the claws ripping through fur and skin, so that pain maddened him, making him witless, and he raced in with a loud bark that Ned heard as he climbed the fell to retrieve his gun and shoot at the plentiful rabbits, now making a come-back after decimation by myxomatosis.

The badger turned clumsily. The dog sprang for his shoulder, and took a grip that in any other animal would have meant a death wound. But Brock's fur was thick, and although he was old, he was experienced and cunning, and he moved quickly as the teeth met, so that the bite was superficial. He shook himself wildly, and twisted, and the dog fell back, puzzled.

Ruff did not lack courage. He circled again, watching for an opening. He wanted the remains of the lamb, and he knew that the badger would not give in easily. As he jumped again, Brock turned and this time the savage paw gashed the dog's head slashing to the bone, cutting wickedly into the vulnerable flesh.

Ruff jumped and found a grip on the badger's neck. He hung on, although Brock shook and stamped and turned and tried to swing away. The dog had gone, instinctively, for the jugular, and he clung grimly with no knowledge of defeat.

Old Brock died game, his eyes glazing as the morning star pricked out of the misty clouded sky. The collie relaxed his grip and lay exhausted, panting with pain, blinded by blood, too weary to claim the lamb that had caused so much trouble.

Ned came upon the two of them, stretched side by side, the lamb's carcase mute evidence of the cause of the dispute. Ruff did not even scent or hear the man, and Ned saw at once that the killer had little chance of living with his own wounds, so that his compunction at shooting a dog was less as he settled the shepherds' problem for them with swift mercy that killed the animal as it slept.

Later that day he took the two bodies to Dai, knowing that

the Vet liked to examine dead animals whenever he had the chance. He would send his findings on the badger to the British Mammal Society for their records. Dai had his own theories about killer dogs, and he did a quick post-mortem on the collie, finding, as he had expected, that Ruff not only had an abscess in his injured shoulder but also a deep-seated tumour in the brain.

That night, sitting in the smoky kitchen at the *Swan*, Ned told of the death of both dog and badger.

'Now the luck'll change,' Josh said, having dropped in for a quick one, wearing his best clothes, that he never wore for handling his animals, and careful to keep clear of the other farmers, who all sat uneasily, half afraid. The All Clear should be given soon, but no one knew if the stag could have carried the virus, and his visits had been widespread, as he was welcomed by all.

The doctor had at last persuaded Mrs Jones to take to her bed, and the Huntsman was officiating, amused by his new role and teased by the men, all of them glad to hear that he was staying among them, and moving into the annex at the *Swan* when his cottage came down.

'All froth, and no body. How did you do that one?' Josh asked with a grin, blowing at his beer.

'It's good enough for you, Josh Johnson,' the Huntsman retaliated, knowing the accusation untrue.

The men were aware of Tanner, sitting glumly in the corner, his drink almost untouched in front of him, as he cast uneasy glances at Josh, who sat with the glow of the log fire, always burning to heat the great copper kettle, shining on his red head. Jess crouched beside her master.

Josh was aware of the glances, and at last could bear them no longer. He was not a man to savour a grudge.

'Damn it, Tanner,' he roared at last, his bull bellow making the older man jump, and shoot a sullen glance out of mean grey eyes that sank unhealthily into a sallow face.

'Have a beer on me, and forget it. Badger's dead. Our luck'll change, you see if it don't.'

Tanner, startled, drank his beer, and accepted the peace offering, moving across to the table, anxious to make amends. He had been feeling badly ever since Dai, vicious with anger, had called in to tell him what his mischief had done to the old mare, Sally, and to Bruton Silver's foal.

The schoolmaster, about to say that the badger's death could make no possible difference, changed his mind and wisely held his peace. He could educate the children. It seemed useless to try to inform the parents, who clung to the old beliefs in a way he found extraordinary in the twentieth century, especially when each man could service a tractor, and mend a car.

Yet he had discovered that Jasper went nowhere without a lump of coal in his pocket as a specific against rheumatism, that Ned had a lucky penny and worried sick if he mislaid it, that Rob Hinney always nailed a horseshoe above the door of the milking parlour, and that Peg Johnson rarely made any statement of future plans without touching wood.

'Bet you ten bob the luck's changed,' Josh said exuberantly, his quick one stretched to yet another pint, his mind on the summer Shows that could still be held. He was sure that the standstill order would be rescinded, now that the badger had gone. No one else would suffer. He was so jubilant that he nearly ordered drinks all round, and then remembered that only that morning Peg had been carping about the bills again, and her face had been sour when he said he was bound for the *Swan*.

Bess Logan, who had called in to take Mrs Jones her meal, and bring her some magazines to read, sent by various women in the village, put her head round the kitchen door, and called to the Huntsman, who went to her, startled, as Bess had little time for him, hating the hounds and fox-killing.

'Been thinking,' she said.

Huntsman waited. Half the women in the village seemed to spend their time thinking. But what had Bess to say to interest him?

'Can't make ends meet,' Bess said, her voice suddenly quick and nervous, not liking to talk about money, but the Huntsman, knowing that she, too, had nothing but her pension, and was kindly minded under her carping ways, gave a sympathetic nod. Behind the door, in the big kitchen that served as the public bar, the men were growing noisy, big with relief at the death of the killer and their ill-starred badger, and lightheaded with the easing of their strain.

'Counting chickens too soon,' the Huntsman said, with a quick nod of his head towards the door.

'Oh, them!' Bess dismissed them with one sharp look. She'd never had much time for men. 'I thought. . . . My cottage is too big for me. Need a lodger. He could be quite private like. . . . ' She stopped.

'Mr Betwick's letting me have the annex,' the Huntsman said uncomfortably, his voice gentle.

'Aye. Mrs Jones told me. Thought of you first, but you and me'd not get on,' Bess answered matter-of-factly. 'Be getting at you for hunting, all the time, and mad on Hunt days. Thought of Jasper. Be a bit of company for me, and he's always been helpful, like. Only . . . ' she hesitated. 'Thought I'd ask, first. Not liking to put it to Jasper straight. Dunno how he'll take it.'

'Better than going into the Home,' the Huntsman said. 'Solve everything, that would. Be company for you, and your paddock'll take his animals, and someone to see out for him, and not on his own in his old age.'

He beamed at her suddenly and impulsively took her hand.

'Put it to Jasper. He'll jump at it. And thank you, Bess. We'll never agree, you and me, but you're a good woman, for all your sour tongue!'

Bess stared at him, and suddenly, fiercely, blushed, before going off to her own home, her mind made up. It had taken a power of thinking, but she hadn't the heart to see old Jasper done out of a place to live in the village where he'd been born. And the money he'd pay would help her out of the Home, too. Not entirely unselfish, she hadn't been, but it was warming to know that Huntsman thought so.

She went on down the lane, thinking. It was mortal lonely, evenings, when you'd neither kith nor kin of your own, and half the village thinking you a cranky old witch. Bess stood at her cottage gate and looked out over the fells.

The heather spilled down them in a mist of purple-blue, hazing the coarse grass, the colour broken here and there by the sharp waxy yellow bloom upon the furze. The land swept up above her, rising, majestic, to Horton Pike, and fell away below her, to the flattened glinting water on Horton Pool. Beyond it, out of sight from where she stood, was Horton Mere.

This was Jasper's heritage, as well as hers. She owed it to him. Been lucky all her life, and he'd helped out when he could. Her thoughts circled, justifying her actions, and then, as the big battered old tom tiger cat came to greet her, back arched, eyes shining, a raucous purr shaking him as he threaded himself against her legs, her face softened, and her hands stroked his thick fur.

'And there's a problem I hadn't thought of,' she said, as she opened the gate that led to her gay little garden. 'How in the world are you and Stalker and Nell going to settle together?'

The cat frisked in front of her, tail held high, his thoughts on food.

CHAPTER EIGHTEEN

BRUTON was coming back to life, and so were all the other villages. Ted Wellans, newly home from Majorca, was resigned and philosophical. The area had been given the All Clear, the standstill order was rescinded, and his was the only herd that had suffered. Rob's suspicions, his own swift isolation, and the Ministry precautions had completely isolated the outbreak. He was glad of that, being a generous man.

'Can't have all the luck all the time,' he told his wife, as they watched the chickens scratching in the dust; so few living creatures left on the farm besides the dogs and cats. The sheep far away on the fells in summer quarters scarcely counted at this time. A few guinea-fowl remained in the far field, and the donkey and the horses grazed in wide empty pastures formerly used by cows.

Rob Hinney had recovered too, though he still felt uneasy when he met Sergeant Henty. The Sergeant was a forgiving and an understanding man. Not like Rob to get drunk and blow his top. Best forgotten, but it was Rob who could not forget.

Mag Hinney had bought all the farming papers she could find. Notices of coming Sales filled them, and the cowman sat in the small cottage which had belonged to generations of Hinneys, and which Ted had modernised, and studied the catalogues.

Jersey heifers. Bulling heifers. Calves, and milkers. He marked the place in each paper, the farms that had bred them, the bulls that had sired them, until he'd built, on paper, as good a herd as they'd had before. It wouldn't be the same, nothing was ever the same, and no bull like Majesty, their two-thousand-guinea pride, but it would be a good second-best. When Ted came home there'd be facts and figures, and Appledale Sale only a week away, and the fields had been empty for over six weeks and safe to stock again.

Rob, his spirits rising slowly, went out into the sunshine and looked at the roses. His elder son was brooding, lying on the grass. Rob grinned, and pulled at the boy's leg, and in a moment the two of them were rough-housing, as if nothing had ever happened to change their lives.

John went off happier than he'd been for weeks as the father swung his youngest daughter high in the air, and then pinched his wife's rump, giving affection and apology all in one gesture, which she understood perfectly.

'Be cows back at Wellans soon,' she said. 'Be good to see them back.'

She picked a large bunch of roses to take to Mrs Jones, who was much more her usual self, now that her work was eased and she could rest her back. There were no summer

151

visitors at present at the *Swan*, and the Huntsman was managing well, putting a brave face on a bad job, regretting his own cottage bitterly, but tidying the annex and fixing shelves. A mood of optimism came to him, and his small whistle was joyously audible. The dogs and cats found his goings-on irresistible, and spent absorbed hours watching him.

He broke off his task when Mag called in, and promised to see to the bar, and went with Ranger high on the fells. He took his horn, too. It had been a long time since the urge was on him to practise, and, as the hound ranged delightedly after the scent of rabbit and trace of hare, the full notes sounded over the village.

'View Holloa. View Holloa. View Holloa.'

Nell raced to the cottage door, barking, and Jasper followed her, looking up over the maze of green and purple, broken by grey rocks, towards the little figure, dwarfed and gnome-like, high above them, his horn ecstatic.

'View Holloa. View Holloa. View Holloa.'

Every hound was baying, the women were at the doors, the men laying down their work, dropping spade and pitchfork, stopping as they toiled in barn and byre and stable, in house and field and garden, in smithy, shop, and store.

Hunting! Autumn was coming, with the fall of leaves in a flame of red and gold, the crisp bite of frost, the tang of wood-smoke from every garden, the slither and slip of paws as the first cub fled over the scree, the hounds, full-cry, behind it, the men, patient, plodding, drab, their lives filled with sudden excitement, the thrill of following, the call of the horn, the View, and the flying pack.

The race against death, with the romping beasts behind, and the little swift sly one in front, ready to fox them, outwit them, twisting and turning, hiding and climbing, running till the moon was a thin thread above him, seeking safety anywhere, in barn and stable, manger and haystack, even on the rooftops, cheating the hunters of their prey nineteen times out of twenty.

'View Holloa. View Holloa. View Holloa.'

Booted hikers stopped to listen. Riders on the bridle paths reined their ponies, and the ponies pricked their ears. Motorists, catching the echo, elfin and magical in the distance, drew in to the verge, and sat, as the horn sounded and sounded again, until the man playing it changed his tune, and Gone Away drifted downwards, followed at once by the long notes of Gone to Earth.

Jasper, his hand on Nell's neck, aware, as never before, of her warmth and gentleness, and of his need of her, his beautiful setter, who would soon have to go to a stranger, listened with a stony face. That was a sound he would never hear again. Grim-mouthed, he went to the cows, and fed them extra hay, to eke out the dry, dusty grass, and then threw food for the chickens, watching them chivvy and chase for it, vying, one with another, as to who should get most, while Stalker, knowing it was more than life was worth to chase the fowl, sat by Jasper's foot and chattered his teeth and angrily twitched his tail.

Bess, coming up the hill with her offer ready but her courage failing, saw Jasper's face as the long calls keened from the fells. She did not know how to begin. Jasper would not take what he thought was charity, and he was uncommon cranky of late.

She paused at the gate, and then, from nowhere, a sudden sharp pain hit her. It had come and gone in the same way before, but this was worse than usual, and she gasped, and Jasper heard her, and turned quickly.

The pain vanished as swiftly as it had come, leaving her shaking, clutching the carefully made gate. There was concern in Jasper's eyes.

'Bess!' He had forgotten his own troubles, and his voice was anxious. 'Come in and sit down, and have a cup of tea.'

She walked slowly, and Nell went to greet her, tail waving with pleasure. All animals took to Bess, whatever people might think of her. The old woman patted the sleek head. Even Stalker weaved deviously against her legs, a throaty purr rumbling deep inside him.

The kitchen was clean and comfortable, the furniture shabby and well loved. Bess sat thankfully in the creaking wicker chair and Nell leaned against her, on the worn old rug that Jasper's sister had pegged laboriously many years before. There was a picture of her, a faded photograph in a dark frame, which stood on the dresser. A hard woman, Mildred Ayepenny had been. Bess remembered her well.

Jasper brought the tea, and looked at her thoughtfully.

'Better?' he asked.

Bess nodded.

'Doctor says I ought to take a lodger. Somebody as would do a bit of wood-chopping and fetch the groceries, and help out,' she said. 'All very well for him to talk. Where does an old woman like me find a lodger like that? And I'm not easy to live wi'.'

'We're both getting on, and uncommon cranky,' Jasper agreed with a brief return of his former humour, and a quick look from under shaggy brows. Not but he could have given Bess near on twenty years and not notice, only a young 'un was Bess, not more than sixty odd, but the rheumatism and a hard-worknig life and no luxury had taken a fair old toll.

'Cottage always was too big for me,' Bess went on, stirring her tea dreamily. 'Vicar says he thinks perhaps some of that furniture of mine'd fetch a big price in the Town, and it'd help. But can't bear the thought of empty rooms.'

Jasper looked at her, his old eyes shrewd, and then suddenly grinned, a gap-toothed mischievous grin that had been missing from his face for days.

'Out wi'it, Bess,' he said. 'What's on your mind?'

'You and me's been neighbours a long time. All my life, and most of yours,' Bess said. 'Know each other's ways, and don't intrude. I could do wi' the money for that old furni-

154

ture, and you could bring some of yours to fill the rooms. Be a bit of cat fighting, I don't doubt, and not only between the cats,' she added, with a sudden pawky grin, 'but it'd settle down. And I do need a bit o' help, Jasper. Not just spinning a yarn to tempt you. The bit extra for your lodging'd help a lot. And I'm a good cook.'

Jasper looked at her over the rim of his tea-cup. It was a solution, and a sight better than the Home. He could keep the beasts, and stay in the village, among folk he knew, go down to the *Swan* o' nights, have a fire of his own where he could toast his old bones, and not share it with other men as old and cranky as he.

He could see autumn come to the fells, and snow lie thick, and the new lambs stagger when winter released its claws; see the summer bloom on the gardens, and the autumn haze, and hear the call of the horn and hound music. It wouldn't be easy, not him and Bess, and it wouldn't be his own place, to do as he liked. A long time since he'd had to study other folks' ways, and Bess had a rough tongue. Like his sister Mildred.

He knew he would pine and die in the Home, without a cat to curl on his bed, or a dog to lie at his feet and call him master. He made up his mind.

'Suit both of us,' he said. 'Might fratch a bit, now and then, but who doesn't? I'll come, and thank you, Bess. Means more than I can tell?'

'Be company for each other if we want it,' Bess said. She put down her cup, scratched Stalker's tattered head, and fondled Nell. 'And I've always fancied cows in the old paddock. Grass is good there. Josh puts the donkey and used to put poor old Sal there, to keep it down.'

'And your geese keep it down come Christmas-time,' Jasper said with a grin, remembering a hiker who had been pinned, terrified, in a corner of the paddock against the hedge while the old gander did his best to make a meal off his boots.

Bess grinned too.

'I'll ask Vicar to help me sell the furniture. He says the cleversticks in town could cheat me. Wants a friend of his to come and look at it. Funny,' she went on, musing over the queerness of things, 'never thought much of the old stuff, and it's mebbe going to bring in a tidy bit.'

Jasper watched her walk down the path, his mind suddenly eased. He looked out of the window, up the fells. Sunlight spilled from between the clouds, flooding grass and heather, furze and harebell with regal warmth, and bringing the sun-starved beasts to bask for a little before driving them to seek deep shade where they could lie panting, plagued by flies, unaccustomed to such favours.

He took his stick and went to meet the Huntsman, who was zigzagging mysteriously down unseen paths, half-hidden in summer-high bracken, walking briskly back to take over from Mag and ready the *Swan* for the lunch hour, and make sandwiches for any travellers that needed them.

'Going to move in with Bess,' Jasper said, as Ranger greeted Nell with a joyous bark, and chased her towards the village. Full of sun-craze, infected by her master's lightening mood, Nell frisked like a two-year-old.

'Fool dogs,' the Huntsman said, his voice warm with satisfaction. Life was good again. He lifted the horn.

'View Holloa. View Holloa. View Holloa.'

The sound awakened the echoes, and the hills flung back their challenge. The two old men walked back to the *Swan*, haloed by sunshine.

CHAPTER NINETEEN

APPLEDALE SALE was the biggest event of the year. Cattle were milked at dawn, the women helping, every hand in every home being used to ensure that all necessary chores were soon finished. The others could wait.

Children were dressed in their best, cars and Land-Rovers cleaned and polished. Horse-boxes drove through the village from sun-up, the more knowledgeable boys running to identify them.

'From Buttonskille. Fred Murray's selling off some of his calves.'

'From Farthingdale. Joss Davis's bull.'

Josh was up early, grooming Rennie's Beauty. The Shire was muddy, having chosen that morning, of all mornings, to roll in a boggy wallow, feeling his youth.

Josh washed him down and began the long patient curry-ing, working like a cavalryman, to a rhythm that he kept in time by a persistent soft whistle that made the horse prick his ears and turn his head, intrigued.

When the Beauty shone with care, Josh relaxed, led him into Silver's empty stable, and tied him firmly, putting a bluff over his eyes to keep him quiet. He wanted to pretty him up, Shire fashion, for the Sale, and he brought the long rib-bons, and small flying red and yellow standards that were to glorify his mane, and began, his fingers nimble.

The Shire bore it well. He was a biddable, curious horse, enjoying life immensely, attached to people, interested in everything that went on around him, from the Huntsman's Siamese cat stalking a field mouse to the bright eyed robin that scolded him from a bush.

He did not like the horse-box, and at first stood four-square, his hooves as firmly planted as if they had roots, his whole body resisting from tense shoulder to sturdy quarters, refusing to enter the dark and unknown tiny claustrophobic space that might hold unimaginable horrors in its depths.

Josh brought the bluff again, fastened it so that the horse could no longer see, and finally persuaded him to trust him-self to the ramp that gave beneath his weight, and the sway-ing floor. The mares were watching, also curious. Silver had her grey-fringed head over the gate, and her fosterling stood beside her, the pair making an odd picture, for the Shire was heavy-built, strong and sturdy, and the foal, half-Arab breeding, was slender and light, an airy-fairy goblin change-ling, close beside her, leaning against the solid maternal com-fort of her body, although the day was warm. The shock of losing his own mother so young had made him follow Silver constantly, lest she, also, withdrew her comfort from him.

Libby, the donkey, and Sensation's foal, Bruton Hope, twice the size of the fosterling, watched too, the foal intensely curious, as the big Shire vanished from his sight. He turned his luminous eyes to stare at Josh as if sure that the man was responsible for this mysterious conjuring trick, and could explain it, but life was destined to remain an unfathomable mystery, and presently the foal tired of trying to puzzle it out, and pushed his head against Libby, who was jostling him.

Peg came down in her best dress and a hat that made Josh whistle mockingly and grin.

'Make it at the Mother's Union, then?' he enquired, as she climbed into the Land-Rover beside him.

'You!' Peg said crossly. 'Got it in Kendal, and well you know it!' She had never dared to tell him the price. Her one extravagance, and she soon regretted it. The guilt remained with her still.

Josh only grinned as he let in the gears. Jasper had promised to keep an eye out for the farm and the horses, lest summer visitors came trespassing and left a gate open. They passed the old man in the lane, and Josh stopped to greet him.

'Mighty spry today, Jasper. Won the pools?'

'Going to move in wi' Bess.' Jasper said, and Josh moved hastily aside as Peg leaned across him, knocking her wickedly expensive hat askew.

'Jasper, that's wonderful.'

'Aye. It is.' Jasper grinned, and stood with Nell beside him, watching as they drove off. He had the farmhouse key, but first he went to look at the stallions, who were out of sight beyond the house. He was proud to be in charge, and anxious to see that all was well.

'Good job we've a beast for sale. Look at that car park,' Josh said, as they drove past the overcrowded field to that reserved for buyers and sellers.

'All those horses!' Peg was looking at the pens and the covered alleyways, and the ponies that were walking, and the hunters that were trotting, showing off their paces, all about the enormous cobbled yard.

The place was noisy with shouting and laughter. A

balloon-seller did a brisk trade, surrounded by mothers with small children. A number of stall-holders had set up shop by the gate, with tools, and rope, and cheap-jack jewellery, mending-wools and elastic. The ice-cream van vied with the hot-dog stall and the man who sold large balls of candyfloss, all froth and colour and bubble, from an ancient van.

Josh went off to find out when his Shire was due for selling, and Peg made her way to the tea stall, where she met a crony. They were soon exchanging year-old-news of their children and grandchildren.

Ted and Rob, eager and excited, were among the cattle, looking at Jersey heifers, arguing amiably, sizing up this one, ticking that one off on their lists, eager to start another herd. The cowman stepped out vigorously, his face redder than usual, his blue eyes bright with enthusiasm, the thought of having cows to handle dominant in his mind so that he could scarcely wait for the bidding to start.

'There's a fine young bull,' he said, coming back to Ted with yet another tick on his catalogue.

Ted went to look at it, and found Josh contemplating a miniature Shetland pony that was no bigger than a large dog, with an expression on his face that would have done credit to a man seeing a Martian for the first time.

'Just think of that beside my Shires,' he said, grinning at Ted, and rubbing his hand against the little creature's shaggy coat. 'No bigger than a Labrador.'

Ted laughed.

'Probably die of shock if you tried it,' he said. And then, thinking of his own affairs, he added, 'going to end up with a herd of five hundred milkers and ten bulls if Rob has his way. See you and Peg at the *Wild Goose*?'

Josh nodded, and went to fetch the Beauty out of the horse-box. He was due for auction just before lunch. The Shire came quietly, and many passers-by stopped to stare at him, and admire his eighteen-hand magnificence, his friendly eyes, inquisitive under long sweeping lashes that a film star might have envied, his whole presence enhanced by the ribbons that glittered against his sleek shining coat, braided decoratively through mane and tail.

'End of an era.' A small man, tripping in a too-long-tightly-belted raincoat stopped to talk to Josh as they passed. 'Built our greatness on the Shires, the old plough horses, the old war horses. And how often do you see them now? Almost forgotten, more's the pity.' He nodded to Josh, a thin-faced man with tired eyes, his trilby hiding his forehead.

Josh recognised him as a breeder of ponies from the Midlands, an odd and determined little character who insisted on seeing a buyer's home and stable and grazing before he sold one of his beasts, ensuring a steady market of people anxious to have one of his ponies as a symbol that their status was right for such a finicky seller.

'Used to plough with two like that,' a big roughly dressed old man said, as Josh came by. Huge calloused hands swept gently down the Shire's neck. 'Rather have a horse than a tractor any day.'

The Beauty listened, using his ears to tell the men that he knew they were there, and he was glad of their presence, among the noise and bustle and frightening strangeness.

'Arr,' the ploughman said, grinning, putting on an act that went down well with summer visitors, who expected their farm labourers bucolic, and often stood him an extra pint on the strength of it. 'Can tell a horse your troubles. He won't repeat them, what's more. You'd look all right pouring out your woes to a tractor!'

He laughed gustily, wiped his hand down the side of his big mottled nose, grinned again, and nodded as he walked off.

Josh led the Beauty into his stall, and stood beside him, talking. He was not going to leave him on his own, not here, among strangers. He could feel the Shire trembling. Sometimes the beasts were tranquillised, often necessarily, but he didn't really hold with it.

Two boys ran down the alley between the lines of horses, and a massive chestnut hunter lifted both legs beneath him and lashed out, missing them by inches.

'Don't do to run where there's horses, lads,' Josh said, grabbing the smaller. 'Scares 'em. You near frightened that big chap out of his wits, coming sudden behind him when he couldn't see you and didn't know you were there.'

The boy looked up at him sullenly, twisted free, and walked away, careful this time to keep well back from the hind hooves that were full of sudden menace.

'In the old days everyone was horse-minded,' the assistant said, coming in with a pot of paste and the number 33 on an oval paper plaque. He patted the horse, and spoke, warning the Beauty of his presence, then dabbed hastily, slapped the number down, and walked on to the next stall. The Beauty twitched his skin irritably at the feel of the treacly liquid, and turned his head, as if wondering what on earth had been plastered on to him. He was not bothered, though. Josh was beside him. The assistant passed on his way back again. 'Wouldn't find lads in those days fooling around like that. No discipline, that's what's wrong. Dunno what the world's coming to.'

A piebald pony in the next stall lifted her head, and stared up, transfixed, at the Shire, which towered above the partition, dwarfing her. He huffed at her amiably, and her owner, a girl, almost in tears, selling her childhood companion so that she could buy a horse that would take her now considerable weight, looked at Josh and gave him a watery grin.

'Know any of the horses here?' he asked, aware of her need for distraction and knowing how she felt.

'That one.' She pointed to the chestnut. 'He's a devil. Here for the fourth time. Seems to get sold regularly, about twice a year.'

'Not surprised,' Josh said, looking at the chestnut. 'Not

163

with a kick like that in him.' It was an ugly horse, clumsily made, with a mean head. A temper, but might make a good hunter, for a man that could manage it.

'And there's a mare, a racehorse. There are some Americans over, and they've an eye on this one. There's a reserve of a thousand guineas on her,' the girl said, with awe in her voice.

Josh whistled.

'Look. She's coming up now. Isn't she a beauty?'

Josh stood on a bale of straw and looked over the partition into the wide lane, between empty sheep pens, in which the horses were showing their paces.

The pens housed people, standing on the bales of straw, sitting on the rails, pushing and jostling to see the little mare as she pranced down the central aisle towards the auctioneer's rostrum, in an atmosphere that was electric.

'Here's our *pièce de résistance*,' the auctioneer said, anglicising the phrase, raising a grin. 'Bred from a Derby winner. Her mother had six foals, and they've all won races. . . . One of them has won every event he entered. Look at her. There's breeding for you.'

Peg, coming in to find Josh, and make a fuss of the Shire, who would, she knew, be bewildered, missed the first bidding.

'Shh!' Josh whispered. 'Come and look.'

'She's perfect,' Peg said, clambering up beside him, to look down the alleyway in front of the auctioneer, just at the back of the Shire's stall. The little black mare pirouetted gracefully, tossed her mane, her eyes aware that everyone was watching her, only too eager to be queen and conquer their attention. She flicked her long tail, pawed daintily, an elegant and graceful creature. A tiny boy in white breeches, black jacket, and black hunting cap came forward and gave her a lump of sugar, and the women all gasped, murmuring small feminine admiration. Josh gave a quick appreciative grin and a cynical head-toss. The auctioneer

164

was clever. A stage manager.

'Fourteen hundred guineas . . . ' The end of the sentence was drowned in the outside noise. The auctioneer's eyes were here, there, and everywhere, watching keenly.

'Fourteen hundred and fifty . . . sixty . . . and seventy . . . '

A whip flashed.

'And eighty . . . '

A programme flickered.

'And ninety . . . '

'Fifteen hundred,' a voice said, a rich twang to it, and heads turned, craning, to look.

'Guineas,' said another voice, equally richly accented.

'And fifty . . . ' the auctioneer's own voice was rising, pitched fever-shrill.

The signal had come from a dark man with an expression of barely contained excitement on his face, every feature alight, eyes dancing. Small, dapper, dressed in dark olive-green trousers, a shining white mackintosh flung back to show the scarlet lining, he looked a buccaneer, out of place among the breeches and hacking jackets, the dark suits of the knackers, the best suits of the farmers, and the oddly gay but ragged gypsies, swarthy-faced who were drawn as irresistibly to a horse sale as a cow to her calf.

'Sixteen hundred guineas.' The voice sang, and a man stood forward, a bull of a man with iron-grey crinkled hair crimped to his skull, a powerful face with a massive chin and determined mouth, a man who would stand no rivals. His clothes seemed too small for his powerful body.

'And fifty . . . '

The crowd had thickened, brought from the outskirts, come to see the fun, catching the excitement, murmuring, whispering, watching, the swarthy gypsies laughing, amazed at so much money, a thin boy with one gold earring swinging against a dirty neck watching with brilliant dark eyes, noting every move of the two antagonists.

'Seventeen hundred . . . guineas.'

The last word was emphasised. The silence was so great that at the far end of the yard a man auctioning oddments of farm tools could be heard.

'Three and six, I'm bid, I'm bid.' The rough voice sang into deep silence, and Peg grinned at Josh.

'Any advance on seventeen hundred guineas? Any advance on seventeen hundred guineas? Going for the first time for seventeen hundred guineas . . . ' The auctioneer looked round at the watching crowd, pausing for effect, his face bright and interested, eager with such good business.

If prices stayed high . . . His dreams were on his commission as he said, 'Going for the second time for seventeen hundred guineas. . . . Gone!'

The hammer flashed down, the showman flourished it with dramatic effect, and the huge man walked forward and took hold of the mare, his eyes eating her.

The silence exploded into incredible noise.

'You won't be sorry, sir,' Peg heard the attendant say, as the man led the mare out. He nodded and darted a curious amused glance at his rival, who merely flicked his whip derisively, as much as to say that his turn would come.

'Bidding's daft,' Ted said, some minutes later, as Josh went out to wet his whistle with a cup of tea and left Peg with the Shire. The tea was dark and bitter-brewed, but it was better than standing dry for the next hour.

Josh nodded.

'Hope the heifers don't fetch that sort of price after lunch.' Ted contemplated a herd half the original size with an air of disfavour.

'Probably just the horses,' Josh said, with a wild hope that made him garrulous. 'Those Americans. . . . Wonder where they come from?'

'Oilmen,' Rob Hinney said, coming out of the wooden shed where the tea was sold, a thick ham roll in one hand. 'Like to bid against each other, they say. One of 'em's after Shires, and the other'll probably run him up for the devil of it. They breed horses as a sideline, both of them, and crazy with money.' Rob always knew the gossip, having more cronies than any other man in the village. 'Might stand lucky, Josh.'

'And might not,' Josh said, to propitiate any gods that might be listening.

'Twenty-one.'

'Horse before mine.' Josh turned and shouldered through the crowd, his red head conspicuous, his beard jutting defiantly. He paused at the end of the alley.

A brown pony trotted down the aisle, a small girl, face set, on her back.

The auctioneer had the bit between his teeth, an audience keyed up from the huge price just paid for the mare, and appreciative of every sally, however poor.

'A lovely little pony, a winner. Put the baby between her hooves, she's so gentle. Come on, lovey, show her off.'

The girl's face relaxed, and she turned the pony, circling skilfully, trotting obediently, the fast hooves clicking on the cobbles.

'Who'll say thirty guineas for a child's riding pony? Prize winner, jumped at several Shows. Lots of pluck. Road-trained, and well schooled. You, sir, you won't regret it.'

'Thirty-five,' said an unidentifiable voice from the dark beneath the roof above the pens.

A pig-tailed girl leaned forward to see who had spoken.

'You, love, now, there's a pretty pony for your Mum to buy, and just the right size for you.' The auctioneer leaned forward, his dark face mischievous, a grin on his wide lips.

'I've a much better pony of my own,' the girl said, with an impudent flick of her head that sent the pigtail swinging. There was a roar of appreciative laughter.

'Little lady's a connoisseur.' The auctioneer's eyes flickered as he looked round the pens.

'Forty guineas I'm bid, I'm bid. . . . Any advance on forty?

167

A bargain. Come on, gentlemen, just right for the kids, and you'll never regret it. . . . '

His voice died away as Josh went to fetch the Shire.

'Want me to take him?' the attendant asked.

'Take him myself.'

Josh led the horse out, and took him to the end of the alley, where there were buckets of water. It was a torrid day and the Beauty was thirsty. He drank greedily, blowing the last drops from his lips, spattering Josh's holiday suit with froth.

'Twenty-two.'

There was a murmur of admiration. The Beauty was regal, his head high, his stance perfect. Every muscle rippled, every inch of him shone as if he had been polished, and he moved proudly. Josh, turning his head, saw Alf Miller in the crowd. There was always something for him at a Sale, but today he'd have extra interest. Josh had promised him commission if he made a profit on the horse. Ten per cent. Alf thought that fair, remembering his own big profit on the Shire that the Huntsman had had to shoot after the stallion had savaged his master. The Bruton Jet. He'd made nearly as much again when he disposed of the carcase.

'Now!' The auctioneer loved his job, and he loved horses. There was immense pleasure in getting a good price for a really good beast, and this was a beauty. Lived up to his name. He could put all he had into his voice and mean every word of it, and his admiration showed with every word he spoke.

'Rennie's Beauty. A winner, a real champion, gentlemen. Three years old. Winning foal at Derby when he was first shown. A winner last year, and a winner this. Only sold because his owner died and Josh here has more horses than he's land for. He's an eye for a horse, has Josh. You want to see the Bruton Shires, if you're keen on the big horses.'

He was looking at the grey-haired American, who had

moved forward and was gazing at the Shire with uncon-cealed admiration.

'Just under eighteen hands. And his father was a cham-pion, too. Rennie's Magnificence. A fine stallion, and this one has his breeding. Unbeaten champion, supreme cham-pion, four years ago, was Magnificence. Now, what am I bid?'

'One hundred and fifty pounds,' the big American said, his voice casual, and Josh swallowed, caught Alf Miller's eye, stroked the Beauty's neck, and almost choked, his thud-ding heart so loud that he wondered that those standing near did not hear it.

'One hundred and eighty.'

'Walk him. Show his paces,' the attendant whispered, and Josh turned the Shire, walked him down the line, and turned again, so that the horse stood nobly, his dark eyes watching the crowds, puzzled, but unafraid, his ribbons gay in the trailing beams that fingered through the pens and lay beneath his hooves, so that he pawed sunshine, his feet gleaming, the silken hair trapping the light.

Josh moved forward slowly, the Beauty pacing beside him.

'Two hundred . . .'

The grey-haired man dared his compatriot to outbid him.

'Two hundred and fifty.' This was a stranger, and a slen-der man walked forward. His hands rested, momentarily, on the Shire's neck.

'You beauty! You beauty!' His voice was intense.

Suddenly the atmosphere changed. The bidding came faster, voice following voice, one using a finger, another a whip, the third a programme, to reinforce bids. The bidding topped five hundred pounds, went to guineas, and soared to seven hundred guineas. Josh felt light-headed, Peg took off her wonderful hat, Alf eased himself farther and farther for-ward, the crowd coalesced, every voice silenced, eagerness and excitement mounting minute by minute, as nobody dared to breathe.

'Eleven hundred guineas.'

It was the man who had stroked the Beauty as if he wanted to take him, there and then, to drag him away. His voice was charged with feeling, speaking the bid, not nodding or beckoning, full of excitement, as he looked from the grey-haired man to the man in the white mackintosh, every muscle tense.

'Going for eleven hundred guineas. Any advance, gentlemen? Going for the first time. . . . Going for the second time. . . . Gone!'

The hammer crashed.

The buyer turned and grabbed Josh's hand and shook it exuberantly, while his two rivals came over to admire the Shire and talk with them. The successful bidder was an Australian, son of a very wealthy man, and his father, who had started life as an English farmer, wanted to found a Shire stud.

The buzz of voices was so noisy that the Beauty backed, and turned to Josh, looking for reassurance. His new owner took the head-rope.

'All right, old boy. I'll take you where it's quiet,' he promised.

'How will he travel?' Josh asked, wondering if he would be expected to pay the horse's fare, which would, he knew, be something in the region of six hundred pounds. Costly business, exporting horses.

'I'll fix all that,' the buyer said. 'I'll take him to my groom, and then stand you a drink, if you can hang on. Then we'll have to go and settle up.'

Josh led the horse outside and there were eyes everywhere, those from the far end of the field, who had heard of the big price paid, running to see the Shire before he went. Josh found himself surrounded by reporters. A camera flashed, and the stallion turned away, worried by the sudden flare. The buyer returned, and led Josh to the car park, where a resplendent new Land-Rover stationwagon stood, with matching horse-box, the groom beside it, waiting.

Josh eyed the man sharply. He wanted to be sure that the Beauty would not be ill-used. Already his conscience pricked him. He hated selling an animal to strangers.

His fears were stilled at once, for the groom looked up, saw the Shire, and an expression of deep contentment settled on his face, succeeded by admiration. His voice and hands were gentle, his movements relaxed, and the Shire had no hesitation in accepting his new handler.

'Burrows thinks like a horse. Reckon he was one, once,' the Australian said, grinning, as the Shire was given a welcoming pat, and a hand-out of carrots, which he munched happily, his mouth orange as he chewed.

Josh was speechless. Even after Alf's ten per cent was deducted he would have more money for the sale than he'd seen at any one time in his life. He could pay off all the bills, and Peg could stop worrying.

He took the Australian to the *Wild Goose*, where half of Bruton seemed to be congregated round the bar. The women were in the lounge, enjoying a chat with their coffee and sandwiches. The noise was tremendous, and Josh was confused by handshakes and back-slaps, while the Australian grinned happily, stood drinks all round, and promised to come and see the Bruton Shires.

'Showing Bruton Grey Cloud tomorrow,' Josh said, giving the horse his full name for once. 'Appledale Show comes day after Appledale Sale. Will you be here?'

'I'll be staying for that. Won't get Burrows away if he knows there's a Show,' the Australian said. 'By the way, can we keep the ribbons? And will you show Burrows how to fix them? Not seen horses fancied up like that before.'

Josh nodded, remembering Mayday Parades, when all the horses were dressed in their best, with polished harness and shining brasses that had taken the men half the night to clean to perfection. The other half had gone in grooming and dressing the horses. There was something of the old excitement back again.

Ted left, pushing his way through the throng, anxious to bid for his cattle. Peg, coming into the bar to find Josh, thought it time to go. Seeing him bemused, she decided to drive home, and let him sit. It was not drink that fuddled him, but pleasure, of a kind and nature that he had never known before. He was dazed and drunk, not with beer, which he had hardly touched, but with the knowledge of security, freedom from bills, and the thought of something akin to prosperity.

They pushed their way through the crowd, whose voices were high above the lowing of cattle and the occasional frightened whinny of a horse. Peg stopped to yearn over a pen full of foals, the smallest backing, terrified, against the biggest; blue eyes wide and wild. It offered him the apparent security of his mother, warm and large, until it turned and nipped his cheek so that he bolted to the other side of the crowded pen, shaking, making a small commotion of hooves and jostling bodies.

'Best be going,' Peg said, tearing herself away, looking back reluctantly, savouring the heady exciting smell of clean horse and clean cattle.

Josh went to find Alf, but he had vanished, busy celebrating his own windfall in the *Wild Goose*, as unbelievably astounded as the red-headed farmer had been.

'Come on,' Peg said, suddenly afraid that her husband might buy himself another dozen horses, or lose the cheque that was now tucked safely in his wallet, or even lose the wallet to one of the quick-silver-fingered gypsies, still prowling among the pens.

'We'll win all the prizes tomorrow.' His voice was exultant.

Peg looked at him, exasperated, and turned her attention back to the road again. Would he never learn?

'Hold yer whisht, man, do,' she said.

CHAPTER TWENTY

BRUTON was awake before cock-crow. Even the Vicar found himself, long before Matins, standing beside Rob and Ted, admiring the new Jerseys, that thronged Wellans' fields, laying the ghosts of Sheba and Dulcibel, of Clarabel, and Jezebel. They had been delivered late the night before, and were restless in their new surroundings, so that nobody near slept well. The Vicarage garden backed on to the cow field.

It was a grey dawn with a thin drizzle, but a promise of fine weather later.

'It's good to see the cattle back again,' the Vicar said, and Mary Wellans, hearing his voice, went back and changed her clothes, and slipped across to Matins, to offer up her own thanks.

Rob could not wait to be among the cows again. His hands stretched out of their own accord to examine this one, to gloat over that one, admiring the delicate ears and the *café au lait* coats, the dark heads and enormous watchful eyes, brown and secret as a peaty pool.

'Have to name them,' Ted said, listening to the church bell as it rang for the early morning service. There would be a few there, in the dark and peaceful church where the stone crusaders stared blindly at the vaulted roof. Swallows nested in cracks in the pillars, and reared their young, untroubled, coming in through hidden holes high in the roof, for which there was a fund which would, one day, have enough money for much-needed repairs.

All of the cows had pedigree names, long names, and handsome names, but who in his senses would call a cow 'Magenta Martian Rose' when Rosie suited her better, and nothing could be made of Chrysanthemum Queen, except Queenie, or perhaps Chrys.

'Goddesses' names, too,' Ted said, chuckling. 'Had a look last night. We've Rosie and Queenie, true, but we've also got Venus and Aurora, and Diana and Daphne. And Chloe and Phyllis.'

'Cor!' Rob said. He scratched a friendly nose that stretched inquisitively towards him. 'Well, this one's Pansy. Got a look in her eye just like old Pansy Grey that keeps the shop at Willow Corner.'

Ted laughed.

'Better not tell her,' he said, and went, light-hearted, to meet Mary as she came back from the church to get breakfast.

At Bruton Josh had risen long before, and groomed the Cloud until he was burnished. The sun struck steely glints from his coat when he walked out into the yard, into the first rays that broke through a sky that had changed from the dull hues of night to molten metal, and then cracked to show blue promise and brightness.

Peg, the milking finished, pushed the last cow back into the field and closed the gate. She had cooked an enormous

174

piece of home-cured ham two days before, and breakfast was simple, a few giant slices for Josh, a slice for herself, and new-baked bread.

Josh drank his coffee hastily, and went out to braid the ribbons into the Cloud's mane and tail. His fingers were busy with long shining streamers of red and gold and white, when the smart green Land-Rover and matching horse-box drew up at his gate, and the Australian who had bought the Beauty climbed down, followed by Burrows, the groom.

'Nothing's wrong?' Josh asked anxiously, his busy fingers pausing, wondering if the Beauty had come to grief overnight.

'Not a thing. More we heard of your horses, the more we wanted to see them,' the Australian said. 'My name's Lucas, by the way. Dick Lucas.'

Burrows was already in the field, eyeing the mares, looking at Sensation curiously.

'Burrows' Sensation,' he said. 'Isn't she?'

'You know her?' Josh said, looking hard at the groom.

He nodded.

'My grandad's horse. Recognised that odd patch on her withers, and the shape of the white sock on her off-hind. We've lots of photographs of her. I grew up here. Don't you remember, Mr Johnson? Dave Burrows.'

Josh did remember him, suddenly, a tow-headed, snub-nosed impudent youngster who played truant from school time and time again just to be with horses, anybody's horses. Unable, ever, to keep away.

'Aye,' Josh said.

'We wrote to Mr Burrows, or rather to his executors,' Lucas said, looking at the mare, 'but she'd already been sold. If I'd known you had her I might have gone for her instead of the Beauty. Can't manage both, more's the pity. We've several mares at home though, but no good stallions.'

'Where is the Beauty?' Josh asked, wondering.

'Stabled on the farm near Windy Corner. They said they

had room to keep him till we are ready for sailing.'

Josh nodded satisfied. That would be the Bury place. Jim Bury was clever with horses, although he had sold his own some years before, finding them an expensive luxury.

Burrows was braiding the Cloud, his fingers slow and careful.

'Used to do this when I helped me grandad,' he said. 'It's coming back.'

Two more horse-boxes drew up in the lane, and Josh stared, startled. The grizzled American and his dapper antagonist climbed down from the passenger seats, and came through the gate, leaving the drivers with the vehicles.

'Heard you'd only one horse-box, and thought maybe you'd like to show your other Shires. They reckon you stand to win all entries, down in the *Wild Goose*,' the big man said, his mouth relaxed in a wide grin as he took in the trim farmhouse and the immaculate cobbled yard, enhanced by the gleaming stallion, immobile and statue-like, a patient giant, suffering Burrows' busy hands.

He walked over to the field, saw the mares, and whistled.

'I want a mare,' he said. 'Want her badly. Will you sell me one?'

Josh looked at him, looked at his mares, hating to part with them, feeling he had enough money to make him rich for life, yet thinking of lean times to come again.

'I'll equal the price that Lucas paid for the stallion yesterday. And she'll be well cared for, I promise you.'

The dapper man was talking to the Cloud, who favoured him with a dipped head, a glowing look from his wise dark eyes, and the gentle movement of listening ears. The Cloud loved voices.

'Dunno.' Josh was bewildered. It was too early in the day to make big decisions. 'Peg?'

Peg thrust a comb through her thick fair hair, and ran downstairs, having changed hastily when she heard strangers in the yard.

'Mr . . . ?' He looked interrogatively at the grizzled American.

'Nichols. And this is John Dennet.'

'Mr Nichols wants to buy Sensation.'

'Our Polly?' Peg looked at the mare. She had a very soft spot for her. The foal was growing daily. He was crazy now with the joys of summer, and rolling frenziedly, his long legs kicking wildly.

'She's exactly what I want. I breed horses, powerful hunters, and police horses for the Mounties. Sell them across the border. A Shire crossed with a hunter is fine for police work. They've tried it over here.'

Josh nodded, remembering reading about a man who had bred a whole number of horses that way, and the police found them ideal. Power and personality plus courage and docility.

'We'll still have her foal, Peg,' Josh said.

Peg nodded. She would be sorry to lose the mare, but it was too good a price to turn down, and she'd be going to a good home. Not as if she were one they'd reared from birth. She liked the American. You could always tell a man who understood horses. And goodness knows, they'd be fools to turn down the money, the way things were.

'Mr Wellans thought you'd like a chance to show all your Shires, or at any rate, the stallions, your mare, and this foal. We came over to see. We'd like to help. Be something to talk about at home.' Nichols was explaining to Peg, having seen her questioning glance at the horse-box.

'None of them are ready, and there's entrance fees to fix,' Josh said, looking at the mud on Silver's legs, the dusty coat of the foal, thick with grass seeds. Pearl was not ready for showing. Lacked presence. She'd come on, but not for a year or two. She was not as good as her mother, not by a long way, and a bit of a disappointment to Josh.

'Many hands,' Lucas said, taking off his coat. 'Mr Wellans

said he'd see to the fees. You can pay him later.'

And pay him that cheque for Sensation, and he'll have commission on her. Over a hundred pounds. Good thing for Ted he hadn't paid the debt, Josh thought, bemused, pondering on the queer way things could turn out.

He brought the Shires into the stables, and they started grooming, putting bluffs on the stallions so that they should not be awkward or bothered by strangers. He started grooming the foal himself, surrendering it when Ted arrived, full of himself and his cattle, pleased that his good idea and desire to help a neighbour was working out. Time Josh had some good luck. As he groomed the restless little animal, he told the visitors about the badger, and the ill luck they'd had, all summer long.

'Time Josh had a bit of luck' he added, as the last horse-box drew away from the gate, and the Australian nodded. Burrows had taken the Sable, and he himself was driving with Ted, and Bruton Ebony.

The sky was clear, the sun brassy by the time they arrived. The Shires were being shown in a field shaded by overhanging trees, and already a number waited patiently, grateful for deep shadows.

Josh watched as his own were unloaded. They had put in a rare bit of fast work, and the stallions gleamed, the ribbons glittered, the harness shone. Bruton Sable. Bruton Grey Cloud. Bruton Ebony. He had brought Silver himself, and now Ted was leading the foal.

The Australian looked across at the Betwick entries and whistled. There were four stallions there. Betwick Brigadier. Betwick Major. Betwick General. And Betwick Colonel. All veterans at the Shows. All champions. All handsome blacks with white socks and silken hair that glistened in the sun.

Josh looked over to the other side, where Paget waited with Poppet, Peach, and Popinjay, and beyond him were the Green horses, Green Ginger, Green Glow, Green Grace, and

Green Glory, all splendid.

The sound of a fairground organ dominated the noise, the catchy whirly tune clangorous above the shouts of children, reminding Josh of a time, years before, when two of his Shires had been matched against a traction engine and given it best, drawing fantastic loads across the tan. A blaring voice called attention to hot-dogs, and the lilting chimes of an ice-cream van clashed against a roar of applause from the field where Sue Wellans had just repaid her father's coaching by winning first prize with her new pony, Timothy-boy.

Josh realised suddenly that, in the first judging, his horses would be in a different class from the brewery horses. He had only to compete against Shires born in the past three years. He looked at Bruton Hope, dancing impatiently as Ted held him, and he knew with utter certainty that none of the other foals could beat him, anywhere in the field.

The Judge was waiting, a small man with wise eyes, and a knowledge of horses that no one in the country could beat. He came forward now, limping slightly diffident, aware of nothing but the magnificent beasts lined up in front of him, under his critical gaze.

Josh held Silver, who submitted patiently. He had brought the foster foal with her, and Peg held it, her arm against the little beast's warm neck. It seemed an absurd thing to do, but the mare was unhappy away from it. She looked round now, found him near, and settled, well content.

Lucas, his hand on the Cloud, thought he had never seen a finer Shire. He was better than the Beauty, but only marginally so. Every line of him showed his breeding, and he was lighter-built and cleaner-legged than the Green and Pages horses. His feet were perfect.

Nichols held the Sable, his eyes amused, as he thought of himself being part of an English Show. He lived for new experiences, never content to sit back and be idle, and the heady excitement, the raucous fairground music, the bustle

179

of the crowds, and the constant quick-silver movement en-
thralled him, so that his eyes watched avidly, all the time,
never still, looking from face to face, and from horse to
horse.

Dennet was quietly content, amused by the way that he
forced old Nick up yesterday. He had had no intention of
buying, himself, but he could never resist the mischievous
impulse to push Nichols higher and higher, knowing he
could well afford the luxury of throwing money away, and
then dropping out at the critical moment.

Nichols was aware of this, and did not mind. The mare
had been worth every penny, to him, and Dennet did not
know that someone else had been ready to bid should the
price go unreasonably high, so that Dennet, finding his rival
had dropped out, would lose interest and stop. As things
were, he had paid within his own margin, and his stand-in
had not had to bid.

He grinned to himself, amused at his own joke, almost
wishing he could share it with Dennet. The two of them often
travelled together. Sometimes Dennet went beyond all
reason. Sometimes Nichols dropped out and left him carrying the can.

The Shires paced, regal. One by one, they moved slowly
round the ring, showing off their paces, showing the movement of proud strong muscles, the shape of shoulder and
hock and head, the finespun hair on their legs, the broad
brows and noble expression. Lucas, at the rear, dwarfed by
the Cloud, looked at the pacing horses. Breed of giants,
he thought, last of the Great Horses, warrior horses of
England.

Paget led his mare, Poppet. A large untidy man, his
stomach spilled over his trousers top, and the white shirt
was dark with sweat across the back. It was uncommon hot.
He wiped his forehead with a spotless handkerchief, and
checked as the Judge came forward to examine Poppet's
hooves, hidden by the long grass. The mare flickered her

ears, not liking the fluttering cloth.

Waiting seemed endless, and Josh, himself was itchy hot as he stood while the Judge checked the Cloud, seeming to go over him inch by slow inch. He was aware that the Shire shone in the brilliant sunshine, and the ribbons gleamed, and brass glinted. Unaware that his own red head, now sleek with cream, was as bright as the Shire's coat, and that he, with his jutting beard new-washed and silky soft, standing almost as high as his horse, was equally impressive.

The crowd warmed to them. To the giant red-headed man and his great grey horse. The judge nodded, his eyes measuring height and breadth and depth of chest, noting conformation and bearing, seeing that the Cloud was lighter than the old heavy horses, the hair on his legs less, making him easier to look after. A perfect stallion.

Watching the man and the horse, the Judge, well into his seventies, remembered the old days, when several hundred Shires entered every Show, and the farms had them for ploughing and for pulling, and the brewers' drays toiled up the icy cobbled hills, the horses slipping and straining, the men calling and encouraging, and the children came with bread and sugar and carrots and apples and love, gaining something that the modern child would never know.

Josh, standing there, was a sudden symbol, one of the men who made England, who built her fortunes with the horses that brought the imports from the docks and ploughed the land to receive the grain that fed the people. A symbol of days that were older still, when knights in massive armour thundered out on horses almost as big as these, heavy with mail, crashing into battle with clash of steel and thunder of hooves and the frightening background panoply of war.

The horses that pulled the guns.

The living proof of history, of Shires that bred, and whose foals grew and bred again, culminating in those that stood here, the last proud remnant of a breed of giants that many children would never know.

181

He shook his head, and the mists of time vanished, leaving him gazing at a proud man and a regal horse. He smiled, and dismissed them, turning to the Ebony, who had come to take their place.

CHAPTER TWENTY-ONE

THE class judging was ended. Bruton Cloud was winner of the three-year-olds, with the Ebony second. The Sable had won the two-year-olds, with Paget's Popinjay second. Bruton Silver had won the class for mares, and Paget's Peach was her runner-up, while the foal, as Josh had expected, won on every count.

Peg brought sandwiches, which they went to eat in deep shade, while the class judging continued, with Betwick Brigadier beating Betwick Colonel for the championship in his year, and one of the Green mares winning her class. Josh sent Jeannie Lee, who was watching eagerly, to fetch lemonade. It was still uncommon hot.

It was good to sit at ease, in the long grass beneath the trees, while the horses cropped, and a bee droned lazily, and they watched the judge's meticulous examination of each entry. It must have been dizzying for him, under the blazing sun, but he showed no sign of distress.

By the time their meal had ended, and the Judge had left the field for his, Peg and Josh felt that the Australian and the two Americans were old friends, knowing the ranch which Nichols ran in his spare time from working, spare time of which he seemed, to Josh, to have an awful lot; knowing the big ranch on which Burrows worked for Lucas's father, among hundreds of horses, running in herds, bred and sold to the farmers in the outback; knowing Dennet's farm, mostly cattle, but a few horses.

The dapper American collected antiques, and the night before Ted had taken him to the Vicar, who, in his turn, had taken the man to see Bess Logan, hoping that her old furniture might be of interest. Both Bess and Dennet were disappointed when it proved to be reproduction stuff, worth very little, but her disappointment had been alleviated when he found a tiny painted Sheraton table, and offered her fifty pounds for it. She had hoped for much more, but was grateful for small mercies. The table was badly marked where the cat had clawed his legs, and she was astounded that it was of value, the only thing in the house she'd imagined worthless. Funny how things turned out.

'Poor old girl,' Dennet said, thinking of her now. 'The only worth-while thing she had, and she thought it useless and let the cat scratch it!'

The Judge was back, and the class winners were lined up on the field for the final judging. The Cloud tossed his head irritably, surrounded by an aura of flies. It was thunder hot, and all the horses were restless, so that the Judge took pity on them and this time made a shorter inspection. He already knew the result in his own mind, but wanted to check, to be completely fair to each beast.

Waiting for the prize-winners to be announced, in the expectant silence, Josh felt as if he were back at school, wait-

184

ing to hear whether his name was on the list for the First Eleven football team. A lump stuck in his throat and his mouth was dry. The horses must be dry too. Their heads were drooping.

The announcer's voice was quiet. It was difficult to hear him.

'Champion . . . Bruton Grey Cloud.'

There was a singing in Josh's ears. Peg grinned and Dennet tossed his hat.

'Reserve champion . . . Bruton Sable, tied with Bruton Ebony.'

He could scarcely breathe as the voice, dispassionate, went on.

'Champion mare . . . Bruton Silver. Reserve . . . Green Glory.'

And the champion foal was the Bruton Hope.

The sounds were real, Peg was laughing and half-crying, the visitors were slapping him on the back, and Ted was shaking his hand.

'Luck's changed, all right,' Josh said, exuberantly.

'Sshhhh!' Peg said, still not trusting it.

The Judge was standing beside them, smiling.

'An all-out triumph for the Bruton stud!'

There were reporters from the farming papers, and photographers clamouring for the story of the Shires, and of the winners; fascinated by what they had heard of the run of bad luck that had dogged Josh all summer, only to change into such triumph as rarely came to one man.

Peg vanished, not trusting luck, ever. Up one day and down the next, that was life, but it was as well to make the best of it, and the best of their present good fortune, for it might not last. Ups and downs, that was what everybody had, good today and bad tomorrow, and best not call too much attention to the good, lest it vanish, like snow in summer.

Back home, Jasper had already finished the milking for

them, and was cleaning up the yard, and grinned broadly when he heard their news, and saw the red certificates and the parti-coloured ones, and helped undo the ribbons, and feed and water the weary beasts. It had been a long hot day for all of them, and the foal was too tired to eat. He fell asleep, almost as soon as he was put into the cool stable that he shared at night with his foster-mother. Sensation's foal, older and sturdier, fed greedily, and appeared not to miss his mother, who had already gone to share quarters with the Beauty until arrangements were completed for her travelling.

The horses settled, the men found that Peg had made a big meal for them, of home-cured, home-cooked ham, new bread, fresh-picked raspberries, and cream from the farm cows. They finished with bread and farm butter and cheese for which Peg was famous, and always won prizes at the local Shows.

Later the men went off to the *Swan*, anxious to share their victories with Mrs Jones, now up and about, and more than thankful for the Huntsman, who was ready to move in any day. Tonight he was serving the beer, carrying trays, while the landlady rested in her big wicker chair, with cats and dogs strewn round her, in an amiable turmoil that forced the villagers, with great good humour, to pick their way across.

'Funny how the luck changed when Ole Brock died,' Josh said into a rare silence, contemplating the beamy ceiling of the *Swan* and his changed fortunes through a wreath of vile-smelling tobacco smoke.

Ned Foley, quiet in a corner, watching the two Americans indulge in animated arguments over the relative merits of the Green Shires, seeing the Huntsman busy, his former vitality returned, and Jasper in deep conversation with young Burrows, whom he remembered, grinned into his beer-mug. His hand felt down and patted a baby hedge-hog, deep inside his pocket, found near its dead mother, killed on the road. It sucked his finger hopefully.

'What's up with you?' Charlie Dee asked, catching the sly grin and knowing Ned.

Ned was not saying. Only three nights before he had watched a little badger sow trot down the fells and excavate the far entrance of old Brock's earth, now free from the stench of burnt tar. She had worked assiduously, bringing out stale bedding, a long laborious task, armful after armful being dragged to the surface, held close against her chest, and she toiled backwards, snorting and puffing.

Ned watched with delight as she bit bracken and grass and brought it, rolled against her, shuffling clumsily, to line her new home. Just before sun-up she was joined by a big boar, who greeted her enthusiastically. Next year there would be plenty of badgers in Old Brock's earth, but Ned had told nobody but the schoolmaster. He caught Mick Stacy's eye, and saw that the other man had followed his thoughts. Together, they lifted their beer-mugs and silently wished the newcomers well. As if a wild beast could bring luck, good or bad!

'Reckon it was the killer dog did all the damage,' Mrs Jones said, pouring tea for a couple of girl hikers, come in late and put to eat sandwiches in the chilly rarely used parlour, where a blazing fire did little to warm the slippery leather-seated chairs. The Huntsman took the tray in to them as they sat, ill at ease, listening to the noisy men in the bar-kitchen.

'Mebbe so.' Josh brooded over the badger. Perhaps he'd done it an injustice. For all that, he was glad it was dead. Silly to believe in luck, but a man could only judge by what he saw.

It was late when he went out of the *Swan*. Peg had finished seeing to the animals, and he had a momentary twinge of remorse. Poor old Peg. Dull for her all alone while he was at the pub. He went in, to find she had a pot of tea ready, and a secret expression on her face that he could not fathom.

'Look like a cat that's pinched all the cream,' he said at last, puzzled. 'What in the world have you been up to?'

Peg merely smiled, and he lay awake, staring into the darkness, listening to the haunting owl and yelping fox, and the eerie ecstasy yell that he did not identify as badger, wondering what his wife had been doing, that contented her so.

The mystery was not solved until the morning paper came, the farming paper that everyone took in those parts. He washed, and shaved himself after milking, eager to sit and eat and have a quick glance at the headlines.

He read the first page, turned over, stared – and shouted. 'Peg!'

She came, meeker than watered milk.

She grinned at him.

There they were. All his Shires. Splendid pictures of Bruton Grey Cloud and Bruton Sable, of Bruton Ebony, and Bruton Silver. And Bruton Hope, and even Bruton Pearl, running with Binnie's foal beside her, playing tag. And Sensation and Beauty, and the story of the Sale, and the prices that had been paid to him.

Underneath was a full account of his stud, of the bad luck that had dogged him, all summer through, until at last it was changed, and he savoured triumph.

And Peg had more news for him, for during milking five men who had read the paper had telephoned, wanting to hire the Shire Stallions next season. And more would follow. The phone had never stopped ringing since the paper came out. Not local men either. One lived over fifty miles away.

'Who gave them that?' Josh asked.

Peg smiled at him. The reporter, scenting a first-class story, had grabbed a photographer and driven over, delighted to find Peg at home, alone. He spent most of the evening with her, getting the details right.

Josh stared again.

'They're beautiful pictures,' he said.

He took the paper to the *Swan* with him that night, just a look in and home quick, he promised Peg. Showing the paper to Jasper and the Huntsman and Mrs Jones, his pride in the horses was so great that his reeking pipe went out and lay forgotten on the table.

He stood up, his red hair once more wild. The money for the Beauty, and for Sensation, both already on their way abroad, was in the bank, and Peg was busy paying bills, an air of pleasure surrounding her. He had left her at the desk, the three cats helping her, Cappy batting at the pen, Marmie, mad with moondaze, trying to kill an imaginary mouse that he believed was hidden in the middle of an old newspaper, and Tinker, wanting nothing but affection, curled up tightly in her lap, washing himself in uttermost comfort.

Josh had grinned at them and gone, and now his promise to Peg to hurry home was forgotten.

'Drinks all round!' His voice was a trumpet sound, an

exultant flourish, and the village men grinned at him, glad to share his triumph.

'The Bruton Shires!' The Huntsman lifted his mug, his rare smile taking in the room and the men and hounds lying nose on paws, waiting for action. Friendly, smoky, smelling of rank tobacco and beer and men and dogs, the *Swan* had become a haven, and tomorrow he was moving in, without too many regrets for his own cottage. Jasper was moving too. He had many doubts, but at least he would remain part of the village. Make the best of a bad job.

'The Bruton Shires!'

The voices ran through the old building and sounded in the street outside. The hounds, sensing the men's unusual mood, sat up eagerly, expecting that at least a Hunt was to start there and then.

At home, Peg looked at the startlingly large cheque she had received for the story of the study, and planned new curtains. She was going to put it in the bank for herself, and not tell Josh. He spent enough down there, at the *Swan* every night. Time she had a look in. She'd buy a new hat. She'd earned it. And get a hairdresser on to her unruly mop of hair.

Outside in the misty evening the Shires were still, enlarged to giant size by the haze that drifted over the meadows. It was time for them to come in, but Peg watched contentedly, as the mares grazed quietly, foals shadowy beside them, and Libby nudged her jealously, asking for attention.

She went to fetch the stallions, and found them idling, placid, dreaming, and she took them to the stables, quite unaware that underneath their paddocks the two new badgers were lying nose to nose. Soon they would amble to the fells to find good hunting under the moon that spilled its light generously over rock and grass and ferny hollow, and stared down at its own reflected image, gold beneath the silken water of Horton Mere.

ZARA by JOYCE STRANGER

Richard Proud coveted the golden-brown mare from the moment he saw her. Although he couldn't afford Zara, he bought her nevertheless, to breed him winners – foals that would restore the fortune of the Yorkshire stud where he bred and trained racehorses.

Zara was born a winner. She had to be raced and Richard Proud was determined that she should race; but despite personal crises – caused by his reckless wife – a snowstorm that isolated the stud only a few days before Zara was due to run, and an accident to her jockey, he had to find a way to let Zara prove her ability . . .

'Mrs Stranger's understanding of animals is sane and unsentimental, and her picture of the racing community is satisfying.'
– Oxford Mail

0552 09892 2 – 40p

CHIA, THE WILDCAT by JOYCE STRANGER

CHIA – the sound of the wildcat – as explosive as a swear word, as sharp as a slash of claws.

No tame and gentle fireside tabby, Chia is a prowling savage beast who comes out of the night to kill. Often the only traces of her presence are stray feathers and bones, wails and calls in the night.

The wildcat has no friends but many enemies – the most feared of which is man. So Chia makes her home far from human haunts, where the looming shadow and the lethal gun of the hunter will not menace her kittens.

But even there the eagle and the fox give her no rest and the wild cry rings out over the rolling glens – Chia!

0 552 09891 4 – 40p T 54

A SELECTED LIST OF FINE BOOKS
FOR YOUR READING PLEASURE

All these books are available at your bookshop or newsagent; or can be ordered direct from the publisher. Just tick the titles you want and fill in the form below.

CORGI BOOKS, Cash Sales Department, P.O. Box 11, Falmouth, Cornwall.

Please send cheque or postal order, no currency.

U.K. and Eire send 15p for first book plus 5p per copy for each additional book ordered to a maximum charge of 50p to cover the cost of postage and packing.

Overseas Customers and B.F.P.O. allow 20p for first book and 10p per copy for each additional book.

NAME (Block letters) ....

ADDRESS ....

(SEPT 75) OP1

While every effort is made to keep prices low, it is sometimes necessary to increase prices at short notice. Corgi Books reserve the right to show new retail prices on covers which may differ from those previously advertised in the text or elsewhere.